The Butterfly and Other Stories

Panda Books

Panda Books
First edition, 1983
Copyright 1983 by CHINESE LITERATURE
ISBN 0-8351-1021-4

Published by CHINESE LITERATURE, Beijing (37), China
Distributed by China Publications Centre (GUOJI SHUDIAN),
P.O. Box 399, Beijing, China
Printed in the People's Republic of China

CONTENTS

Preface 5

What Am I Searching For? 11

A Spate of Visitors 22

The Butterfly 35

The Eyes of Night 102

The Barber's Tale 113

Voices of Spring 138

Kite Streamers 155

The Young Newcomer in the Organization
    Department 186

Preface

"A land stretching 8,000 *li*; thirty stormy years" is a phrase Wang Meng has frequently used to describe the starting point of his recent fiction. 8,000 *li* is the distance from Beijing to Ili in Xinjiang where Wang was sent to do physical labour when he was labelled a "Rightist" in 1957. The phrase is both a declaration and a defence, for perhaps more than any other contemporary author his work encompasses his own and his country's turbulent history and consequently affords the reader a uniquely personal vision of modern China.

Born in 1934, Wang belongs to the generation of writers who first rose to prominence during the 1950s and who used their work to address and explore the social contradictions of post-Liberation China. His 1956 *The Young Newcomer in the Organization Department* became the subject of an intense criticism campaign in 1957 and was one of the major literary targets of the anti-Rightist movement. Attacked as a destructive, anti-Party, anti-socialist work, the piece produced a nation-wide debate. The story's protagonist, Lin Zhen, is an ingenuous and enthusiastic young Party worker who tackles the inert and apathetic bureaucracy of the District Party Committee office to which he has been newly assigned. Expressed in a straightforward narrative style, the work charts Lin's gradual disillusionment and frustration as his attempts to unseat an inefficient factory manager meet with failure. In the resolution, a rather more muted Lin remains determined to work for the ideals in which he believes, if less optimistic about the speed with which positive results can be achieved. For Wang Meng, the resolution of the campaign against the story was to be twenty years of virtual silence in Xinjiang in the far west of China, from which he was to emerge in the mid-seventies as a mature stylist with a razor-sharp perception and an ability to reflect the society of post-"cultural revolution" China.

Had Wang produced nothing other than *The Young Newcomer*, he would have been assured of a place in modern literary history. Fortunately for readers however, he has chosen to interpret his own and his country's experience through a steady stream of strikingly original works. Although a sense of duty to address issues of social importance remains a constant in his work, the style of his post-"cultural revolution" writing is a world away from his 1950s stories. The shift from socialism as the ideal to socialism as a reality has produced a parallel development of technique in his writing. Indeed, all of the later works represented in this collection demonstrate a thematic and stylistic complexity which is in itself a literary representation of the historical process. Wang believes that the changes, the greater depth and complexity of experience contained within that metaphorical 8,000 *li* and thirty years, requires a change in form itself. Accordingly the later works show a consistent attempt to dismantle some of the conventions of the modern narrative tradition in order to more adequately mirror contemporary society. The earnest confrontation tactics of *The Young New-*

comer have given way to a more mature and reflective approach.

All of Wang's recent fiction is composed of characters, situations, plots and a technique that are emblematic of these thirty stormy years. Nowhere is this telescoping of the historical process more evident perhaps than in the poignant and bittersweet *The Butterfly*, the story of Zhang Siyuan, a high official whose fall from grace during the "cultural revolution" and subsequent rehabilitation are examined through a series of episodes tracing his life from the late 1940s through to the late 1970s. Wang has created a deeply symbolic character in whom the aspirations, the reversals and the resilience of modern China are concentrated. Castigating himself over the suicide of his first wife, Zhang asks, "In 1949, weren't you innocent and young? That was the childhood of our people's republic, the childhood of us all."

One of the great strengths of Wang's fiction is that it is in many ways a literature of questions. Symbolic though they may be, his characters possess an ambiguity and depth not found in some of the more formulaic idioms of modern Chinese writing. Coming to terms with a crushed idealism is an omnipresent theme in these recent work. In *Kite Streamers* two young people, who might indeed as Red Guards have victimized the old cadre of *The Butterfly*, struggle to make sense of a China minus the slogans and banners of their turbulently politicized adolescence. Using an impressionistic technique, the author has woven together a vivid psychological and social portrait of China's urban youth. It is a powerful, personal and again questioning picture and offers a sensitive and genuinely sympathetic perception of a generation finding itself. Despite fairly cheerless employment and housing prospects and after a series of unpleasant episodes in which some of the more negative realities of the new order are driven home to them, the young lovers realize that their strength is in themselves. They resolve to continue their part-time studies, although their chances of acceptance into an institution of higher education are slim. Wang's contention that the traumatic domestic upheavals of the "cultural revolution" can, indeed must, be an enriching experience is reflected in the flinty resilience of his protagonists and his stories usually end on a note of genuine, if rather sober, optimism.

Satire is an important device in Wang's work and in stories such as *A Spate of Visitors* and *The Barber's Tale* he launches powerful acerbic attacks on the classic targets of human folly and moral corruption. Both stories concern themselves with the abuse of official power. *A Spate of Visitors* wryly depicts the sorts of direct and lateral pressure brought to bear on a factory director in order to try and persuade him to reinstate the fired nephew of a high local official. Less indignant perhaps than *The Barber's Tale*, the story again ends on an optimistic note when the stubborn and upstanding director is proved right by turning a hitherto inefficient operation into one that is cited as a provincial model. In the latter story, the narrator, Lü, has worked in a barber's shop at a hotel for senior officials since 1949, and the story, through a series of biographical episodes, encapsulates much of China's recent history. Wang's protagonist guides the reader through the heady idealism of the early 1950s when he was "in love with the new society, the revolution", "deeply loved Marx, Mao Zedong and the Party leaders" and "believed in every

word printed in the *People's Daily*". Trouble begins
in the late 1950s when some of his customers start dis-
appearing and Barber Lü, "not knowing what exactly
were the problems ... still had to join in denouncing
them in political sessions". Barber Lü's humane
response in helping a beaten Rightist official
leads to the final third of the story when he is
invited to the provincial bureau by the now-rehabilitated
cadre. Here Wang commences a lacerating portrait of
the special privileges of an officialdom more interested
in its own material well-being than with the proper
concerns of good administration. He conveys a strong
sense of moral indignation at this trend although the
central character, unlike his vastly more cynical son,
resolves to remain on good terms with the rehabilitated
cadre, demonstrating again a persistent, if tempered,
optimism. Less technically complex than many of his
later works, the story ridicules the limousined-and-
leather-shoed world of high officials alienated from the
people they govern. Lü's resolution to keep the com-
munication lines open with the cadre, "If everyone
avoided them, not telling them what he thought, what
would happen to our country and the Party?", echoes
again the final paragraphs of *The Young Newcomer*.

The particular crossroads at which most of Wang's
characters find themselves is frequently suggested by a
journey in his stories. *Voices of Spring* and *The Butterfly* begin with their protagonists, in both cases rehabilitated cadres, making physical as well as metaphorical
journeys. His characters are placed in fluid, unfamiliar
contexts as they try to come to terms with the heavily
symbolic scenery swirling around them. This use of an
impressionistic, achronological technique provides his

characters with a latitude for reflection which produces a much denser, less mechanical sense of the historical process than straightforward narrative would allow. *Voices of Spring* is one of the most extreme examples of this technique, where the protagonist Yue Zhigeng's splayed vision reflects a China of "sealed boxcars dating from the time of Watt and Stephenson" pulled by a "brand-new, immaculately clean lightweight diesel engine", and, despite the obvious difficulties, expresses a clear-eyed dedication to the daunting task of modernization.

Wang's fiction does not shy away from some of the murkier obstacles to that modernization. *The Eyes of Night,* again with its protagonist moving through a changed and complex landscape, dissects an initial resignation towards and ultimate rejection of petty corruption.

Wang's vision is that of an optimist, a realist, a tenacious idealist. It is a complex vision, attempting to chart an emergence from a trauma, from which a greater understanding and awareness must arise. The importance of his work lies in its ability to convey the dimensions of that experience and to do so through a technique which has evolved as a direct response to it. Wang's accomplishment in using this technique to universalize a powerful personal perception makes him one of the most important literary figures in China today.

Rui An

What Am I Searching For?

One late autumn evening in 1953 on the second floor of a new building not far from Beixinqiao, I, a 19-year-old Youth League cadre cherishing a secret passion, closed the door of my sunless office-cum-dormitory and, beneath the lamplight, started writing line by line on a blank paper pad. Beside me there usually lay a pile of dossiers, unfinished reports and summaries and, if there was a knock on the door, I would quickly place a sheet of paper on top of my pad so as to give the impression of working late into the night. When I first started writing, I felt that I would be a failure and an object of mockery, and that my ambitions far exceeded my abilities.

As I sat at that desk, pen in hand, I was aware that what I was doing would affect the whole of my life. I glimpsed a kind of sublimity, felt a solemnity, profoundly aware that I was striving to record what was, though transient and fleeting, beautiful in life, trying to impose a form on intense, difficult-to-comprehend emotions. Although my writing could in no way convey the rich texture of real life, I sincerely felt that it was the crystallisation of poignant emotions, the sheen on life, that it could bear the imprint of youth, that it was in itself more enduring than day-to-day existence, more able to elucidate that existence to people, that it was an eternally unchanging, undiminished message of the soul.

I felt too that the writer was the luckiest of all people; able to communicate directly with an infinite number of friends, he was never completely alone, and with this affinity was able to create a completely new, happy, just and full existence.

There was a Xinhua Bookstore near the Youth League District Committee where I then worked and I often used to go in to absorb the heady fragrance of printing ink. As I wandered back and forth along the book-shelves, I hoped that I would one day find my own work — my conscience — sitting there.

That was how I felt when I wrote *Long Live the Youth*. It did ultimately get published; not then, but when my own child was older than I had been when I wrote it. Twenty-six years were to pass from its creation to its actual publication, more than a quarter of a century. When it appeared in 1979, I was no longer as excited as I would have been, knowing as I did the kinds of risks and responsibilities a writer must bear, the kind of price that had to be paid — in effort, in tears, in time — sometimes in blood, in life itself.

Because literature seeks a brighter world, seeks to up-hold truth, because it thirsts for development and prog-ress and because it is about human beings, it takes human beings as its core, urges them to live like true human beings and requires that human relationships be as they should be — communist relationships, with the aged and young of others treated as one would treat one's own.* Therefore it must fight against exploi-

---

* A reference to "Liang Hui Wang", *Mencius*.

tation, against darkness and ignorance, and take issue with all the forces and ideologies of reaction and conservatism, with hypocrisy and falsehood. And these same forces of darkness and reaction cannot but regard literature as a thorn in their flesh. While I was still at middle school, I became familiar with the names of writers who had been executed by these forces, writers like Rou Shi, Yin Fu and Hu Yepin.* And during the ten ruinous years of the "cultural revolution", I was constantly astonished by the intense, instinctive, even bestial, nature of Jiang Qing's fear and loathing of writers.

My first teacher of literature was my aunt — she came to visit me in 1967 when I was living in Ili in Xinjiang and sadly passed away a few days later as a result of a cerebral haemorrhage. I will always remember how, when I was a seven-year-old second grader, she took my first "essay" on spring wind and completed it with the maxim; "Let the wind dispel the darkness from this land!" My teacher, who never seemed to doubt for a minute that this could be the work of a seven-year-old, enthusiastically underlined it in red to show her approval.

Truly, literature must act as a wind to dispel the forces of darkness, must nurture the hundred blossoms and arouse the swallows and the larks. It was precisely to dispel this darkness that when I was young I joined the revolutionary movement led by the then-underground Party organizations against Chiang Kai-shek and the Kuomintang. In my youth I became one of the Party's fighters. In the student movement, literature

---

* Writers executed by the Kuomintang in Shanghai in 1931.

was the bugle call of revolution. The works of Lu Xun, Ba Jin and Ding Ling, as well as *How the Steel Was Tempered, Cement, The Ballad of Li Youcai, The White-haired Girl, Heroes from Lüliang District, The Story of a Pail* and *My Two Landlords* were circulated in KMT-controlled areas. I have always believed that works such as *How the Steel Was Tempered* have nurtured a generation, several generations, of revolutionaries in China, the Soviet Union and the world.

I have always believed that literature and revolution are inherently indivisible. They have a common goal: to destroy the old order and let the red sun shine over the earth.* Literature is the pulse of revolution, its signal, its conscience. And revolution is literature's guide, its soul and its source. Therefore *How the Steel Was Tempered* nurtured several generations of revolutionaries primarily because it was the crucible, the ideals and practice of revolution that nurtured it and its author, Ostrovsky.

Consequently when, in the name of revolution, a grandiloquent, specious rhetoric was used to cripple literature, to rape and destroy it, I felt torn apart, felt my body and soul rent in two. My whole being was split: to be loyal to the revolution you must betray literature; if you loved literature and created it, then you were a traitor to the revolution.

Almost every political movement since Liberation has commenced with a literary offensive. The day finally came when I myself was to be a victim of one of these.

As a result, I "consciously" tried to negate litera-

---

* From the Chinese version of *The Internationale*.

ture, to cast it aside and began by negating myself. "You and your writing are worthless and despicable!" I tried hard to believe these utterances at criticism meetings, delivered as they were in deafening tones and with the force of justice. I did indeed discover a worthlessness in a literature incapable of replying to the clamour raised against it.   I wanted to discover the contemptibility of literature, after which I could retire in peace to the resting place indicated for me — the rubbish bin of history. If, after destroying the literature I loved, a "new era of literature", embellished with revolutionary rhetoric, emerged; if, after consigning me to the rubbish bin, China became a purer, better, happier place, how could I not but comply?

And so I heartily acclaimed the phrases, "I'm coming! Mountains and hills move aside!", tried hard to grasp the meaning of expressions like "Soar up to the heavens", "man can conquer nature". Mock me if you will, but my political consciousness grew slowly; instead of opposing them, I tried my best to comprehend the "three prominences",* the "sublime and perfect image", despite the fact that subconsciously I so thoroughly detested them, that I cried in my dreams and soaked my pillow with tears.

During this period a sacred, eternal and glorious literature really did become worthless, enfeebled, pitiful, trampled. It became nothing more than hack scribbling: nothing more than self-deceiving nonsense, a lackey of

---

* A literary formula advocated during the "cultural revolution" which called for emphasizing the most heroic and most positive roles in an opera and the most positive and heroic aspects of their characters.

authority, less than a tuft of hair on some VIP's skin. Alas, literature, goodbye!

Literature predictably became despicable, full of lies, deceptive and anaesthetic, an opiate brewed in a thieves' kitchen, the executioner's mask, a slanderous conspiratorial device.

Not only in literature, but in life too there was so much bluffing, so many despicable people and events. In the face of all of this, I became mired in despair. I lacked knowledge, power, courage and just marked time, just waited. During those twenty years from 1957 onwards, when I was accused of being worthless and despicable, I came gradually to feel that the accusations were true.

At the same time I came to know true greatness and nobility of spirit. At the bottom of the social scale and in the most distant of places, I experienced the joys and misery of ordinary people and saw from their perspective the chicanery of those years, the arbitrariness of power, saw who was right and who was wrong, the victors and the vanquished, as clearly as one would see a raging fire.

This reversal and failure tempered and enriched us. At last, in October of 1976, what was destined to happen, the event people had long been waiting for, finally happened. History is at one and the same time merciless and compassionate. We liberated ourselves for a second time, because it is a law of history that people must liberate themselves, and if they do not succeed at first, then they must try again.

Like a corpse raised from the dead, order was resurrected from chaos. I was rehabilitated and was once again recognized as a member of the Communist Party, shouldering that heavy responsibility, following that tortuous path. Revolution and literature were reunited and my spirit and character were reunited as well. My literary world was rescuscitated. A formidable task lay before me; to find myself. To find, in the boundless ocean of life, of time and space, of literature and art, my own place, my fulcrum, my own themes, materials, form and style.

For, no matter how much I hailed this second youth, wanted to begin again at twenty-three, to retrace those footsteps of twenty-four years earlier, I was now in my forties. Memories of childhood are beautiful and moving but one can never be a child again. When I look back at *The Young Newcomer in the Organization Department* and *The New Year*, they still produce a slight sense of anguish, a bitter smile, a sense of aspiration, and at the same time I feel a kind of remoteness, as though they belong to another, distant world.

When I was twenty, life and literature were for me an innocent and pure young girl and my work verses offered in the first flush of love. The poetry of love is moving perhaps, but in the final analysis, far, far from adequate. Now, life and literature are for me a solemn, capable and kind mother. Her wrinkled brow shows how she stood fast in that storm, rose from the ashes, how she fell victim to a whore and a witch; nevertheless, her warm bosom is still pure and soft, overflowing with the milk of human life, with a broad and profound love.

No matter how many well-intentioned readers want me to retain the style of the "organization department's young newcomer", it is both impossible and unnecessary. It is more than twenty years now since I was expelled from the "organization department" and I am no longer "young". What I have gained is still more than I have lost; a vast field in which to use my talents, an ability to face the world and brave the storms: twenty years of experience. A land stretching 8,000 *li* — the distance from Beijing to Xinjiang — and thirty stormy years: that is my point of departure now. If my short stories *Bolshevik Greetings, The Eyes of Night, Voices of Spring* or *The Butterfly* all encompass a broader context in space and time, then that is the reason. Those who study literary technique may shake their heads at me, but I will always remember, weep over and laugh at that 8,000 *li* and thirty years, the true fulcrum of my stories.

I am still loyal and devoted to youth, to love, to life, and to the principles and ideals of revolution. Some say that my present style is so different from the past that it would seem to be by another person entirely. That is not the case. The truth is that it has become more realistic, for I have seen the difficulties of life, seen that anything good must grow to maturity, must temper and perfect itself and must undergo trial after trial. That is why, in *Kite Streamers*, for instance, with its romanticism and seeming transparency, my love songs contain a note of sobriety and detachment. In order to sing the praises of this vast ocean-like mother, still brimming with life despite all that has happened, I must use a full and harmonious symphony; my song can no longer be the serenade of youth.

It's true that the forty-six-year-old author is much more sophisticated than the twenty-one-year-old, and although I now exhibit an acrimonious and lacerating contempt in satirizing all of these negative events I have also come to understand that "the real is the rational".* I have come to understand and stress fair play, forgiveness, tolerance and patience, to stress stability and unity. In the acrimony there is warmth, in the fierce sarcasm understanding and behind the bitterness a fervent expectation. I have come to understand that people must have ideals and that ideals cannot be realized overnight. I know too that using literature to influence life is easier than solid, hard work. That is why my writing now lays stress on stimulating my readers, on encouraging and consoling them, rather than on just exposing contradictions and forcing resolutions of social and political issues. So, although in *Bolshevik Greetings* and *The Butterfly*, tragic events are described, I didn't purposely single out anyone for blame. Although *A Spate of Visitors* was extremely pointed, none of the "visitors" was attacked. Xiao and the once-beautiful actress were not portrayed as negative characters. I still expressed absolute sympathy for them.

One young reader travelled a great distance to see me and asked whether or not, after all these years, I myself hadn't become a little like Liu Shiwu.** It was a difficult question to answer. Zhao Huiwen criticized Liu saying: "He's seen it all and he knows it all. . . . He doesn't have any strong feelings left either way." It's true that over these last decades I have seen and learned a few things and that I try to look at problems from all sides in order to make my work more comprehensive, more realistic and more profound. But I am

---

* Hegel: "The real is the rational and the rational is the real."
** See: *The Young Newcomer in the Organization Department.*

still pondering, still feel love, still dare to confront sharp and complex social contradictions.

My hatred too has its limits. The control of this hatred is an essential condition for sustaining and developing stability. At the same time I am certainly not unfeeling or apathetic and have discovered the weapons of satire and humour. In the preface to *Anecdotes from Department Head Maimaiti*, I posited humour as an essential element of existence. In the department head's so-called "humour" is a degree of sadness, an understandable "Ah Q" ingredient. Absurd laughter is a kind of protest against an absurd existence.

A friend of mine told me that he didn't like my laughter, saying that he felt I used it to cover up the contradictions and the pain, to smooth away the rough edges. Is this true or not? Readers may judge for themselves. I honestly feel that we have cried too much and that we have the need and indeed the right to laugh. I feel too that laughter is a higher and more complex form of expression than tears. Animals can cry (as lambs do before the butcher's knife), but only human beings can laugh. Therefore even in my most controlled, serious and sentimental works there is still laughter. I want to achieve the same kind of serious edge as, say, cartoons or theatrical farces are able to do.

A more complex dimension of experience, thought, emotion and life requires a more complex mode of expression. In my work now I try to use several narrative threads, to create something in the nature of a synchronic structure instead of sticking strictly to a single thread. In order to fully reveal that 8,000 *li* and thirty years, to lay bare the relationships and contrasts in all that happened, I have tried to use a kind of "psychological description" to break spatial and temporal boundaries.

My quest, in Chinese and foreign works, classical and modern, is still to find a means of expressing my identity in my own creative work. I am not denying that there are other influences, not merely from foreign literature but from the poetry of Li Shangyin and Li He,* or from the *xiangsheng* comedians Hou Baolin and Ma Ji, but my style still comes from the earth beneath my feet, from the reality of our lives. It is because life in China has become more complex, its tempo increased, that the themes and rhythms of my stories have changed accordingly. Have I found my identity? Have I succeeded? Perhaps I am still groping about, still experimenting. Perhaps I have yet to write what I really want to write. Perhaps I never will.

I think I shouldn't say more. Since the spectator always sees the game best, I would ask readers not to categorically accept the writer's explanation of himself. We must not adhere rigidly to stereotyped literary forms. The right to interpret and dissect literary works belongs to the readers and it is up to them to draw their own conclusions.

Wang Meng
January 1980

Translated by Rui An

---

* Tang-dynasty poets.

A Spate of Visitors

Who Was He?

HE was so keen on efficiency and saving time that after going to the liberated area he changed his name to Ding Yi(丁一), three strokes in all. However, during the "cultural revolution" he, too, came under fire.

There was nothing special about his appearance or voice, and he wore his cadre's blue gabardine jacket all the year round. So some people were afraid that even his wife would find it hard to spot him in the crowd of customers in a department store. Fortunately he had two minor characteristics — it seems no one can be quite free from distinctive features. One was the bulge at the back of his head, the other his frequent frown. His critics had attributed the bulge to "a reactionary skull", the frown to his negative outlook.

He was bull-headed. In the countryside it was the unwritten rule to keep two separate accounts. That for the beginning of the year contained a plan, quota, guarantee and grandiose statements; that for the end recorded the yield, the amount of grain stored and sold to the state and the value of output. The two accounts were never compared or checked to see if they tallied. But this was not Ding Yi's way. He insisted on comparing them and investigating any discrepancies. It wouldn't have mattered if he had just ticked off the cadres in the production brigade and commune, but he took the accounts with him to the Party committees in the county and prefecture to protest. This happened in 1959. All of a sudden the situation grew tense as everyone there woke up to a sharpening in the acute, complex class struggle. Not only was he denounced and labelled a "Rightist", but all the ex-landlords, rich peasants, their children and grandchildren as well as those Rightists who had been sent from the provincial capital to do physical labour in the countryside were reinvestigated and forced to make a clean breast of their relations with him.

Ding Yi's position went from bad to worse.

However, a settlement always comes in the end. In January 1979, Ding Yi was rehabilitated, and in June that year, thirty years after he joined the revolution, when he was more than fifty, he regained his Party membership and was appointed director of the county's Rose-fragrance Paste Factory.

Many people congratulated him, but he frowned and asked, "What for?" Others told him they thought he deserved a higher position; but without hearing them out he turned away. Yet others said that he had grown cocky again, having never really tucked his tail between his legs.

He made his rounds in the small factory day and night, his jacket often smeared with paste which smelt quite unlike the scent of roses. When his wife called him a poor wretch he only smiled.

So, he had very few visitors.

Ding Yi Stirs Up a Hornet's Nest

At his new post Ding Yi discovered two big problems. Here, the word "discover" is hardly appropriate, because these two problems were as obvious as lice on a bald head. They made him frown and rack his brains every day. First, there was no proper control of the by-product of paste, gluten, which the workers divided among themselves to sell, give to friends or exchange for other goods. This was scandalous. Secondly, the labour discipline was so lax that the foreman sometimes tripped over people sound asleep during their work shifts. So, after consulting everyone concerned, Ding Yi drew up a set of regulations and a system of rewards and penalties. In fact, these were nothing new, just standard practice.

A month went by. In May, Ding Yi decided to make an example of a contract worker named Gong Ding. For one thing, this young man had stayed away from work for four months without asking for leave. For another, he came bold as brass to the factory to demand gluten, and if given none cursed or beat the man in charge. Furthermore, he turned a deaf ear to reprimands. So Ding Yi asked the Party branch committee, Youth League committee, trade union, personnel office and all the other departments to discuss Gong Ding's case. Though he prodded them three times a day, it took them a month and a half to agree to his proposal that this recalcitrant worker should be dismissed. On June 21, an announcement was put up in the factory: In accordance with regulations, Gong Ding's contract is terminated.

Some people knew that Gong Ding was a distant relative of Li, first secretary of the Party's county committee and felt it was a mistake to fire him, but they did not like to say so. After all, he was only a distant relative. So, the decision was finally reached and announced.

Psychological Warfare Breaks Out

Three hours after the announcement was put up, Ding Yi began to have callers. The first was Old Liu from the Party's county committee office. Fifty-seven years old, with an affable expression, he prided himself on his diplomacy and good relations on all sides. Smiling, he put one hand on Ding Yi's shoulder. "Listen to me, Old Ding," he said. "You've worked hard and run the factory well. But as for Gong Ding's case. . . ." Lowering his voice he explained Gong's relationship to the first secretary. He added, "Of course, this has no bearing on his case. You're right to take disciplinary action. Secretary Li would be grateful to you if he knew. It's you I'm thinking of. You'd better not fire him. He'll still have to stay in China, in our county if he's kicked out. We'll still be responsible for him, and he's bound to ask Secretary Li for help. So, better let him off with a warning." He reasoned so earnestly and patiently that Ding Yi began to waver. Just then, however, Zhou, head of the county industrial bureau, rang up.

"What's come over you?" he bellowed. "Why pick on a relative of the Party secretary to make an example of? What are people going to think? Revoke your decision immediately!"

"No, the decision stands!" replied Ding Yi loudly as he hung up the receiver. His face grim, he turned to Old Liu and said, "Outrageous!"

However, visitors kept coming. At dusk, Old Zhao,

chairman of the county revolutionary committee, arrived. Zhao had worked in the county since land reform. He was most influential and strongly entrenched. With a certain reserve he shook hands languidly with Ding Yi, then paced the room while issuing his instructions, not even glancing at Ding.

"We must be prudent, mustn't oversimplify issues. Nowadays people are very sensitive. Gong Ding's dismissal would cause general dismay. In view of this, it's more judicious not to fire him."

He said no more, thinking this directive sufficient. He had paced the room slowly enunciating each word, as if weighing and savouring it. Yes, to him his words were as tasty as spiced beef.

When Ding Yi went home after dark, his wife also poked her nose into his business. Of course, she scolded him out of wifely concern.

"You perishing old fool! Don't you see what you've gone and done? Has messing about with paste all day made you soft-headed? You stick to principles? Why aren't you a member of the politburo? Remember the bashing you got in 1966? Your principles not only got you into trouble, but me and the children too."

This outburst stemmed from bitter resentment and love. And the tears she shed were more eloquent than words. Ding Yi sighed, and was just about to reason with her when in came another visitor. It was Young Xiao, who had befriended Ding Yi when he was in disgrace. Young Xiao had studied in the Philosophy Department of Beijing University where he was labelled a Rightist. Later he had managed to get a job in the county's electricity company. Recently, after his name was cleared, he had been promoted to be a buyer. He was short, big-nosed and extremely ugly. But the more pressure put on him, the more cheery, quick-witted and engaging he grew. His motto was: If someone slaps your face, turn the other cheek. He reckoned that this tactic succeeded three times out of four.

Young Xiao's arrival filled the house with laughter. The first thing he did after taking a seat was to finish up the dumplings left by Ding Yi and his wife who had lost their appetite. Then he asked after everyone in the family, saying admiringly, "How lucky you are to have so many relatives." Next he told them that he would soon buy and send over the TV set, a real bargain, they had long wanted. Finally he related various funny stories about their county, China and other countries till the whole family was roaring with laughter.

"Why aren't you a cross-talk actor?" Ding Yi asked.

"I don't want to do Hou Baolin* out of a job. He's my uncle on my mother's side, you know."

There was another roar of laughter.

Young Xiao took advantage of this to launch his offensive. "Why, there's a small matter I nearly forgot," he said. "It's about that young rascal Gong. He's a real shit! I'll dress him down next time I see him. But Old Ding, you mustn't go too far. You and I haven't got much footing here. Nor do we have powerful backing or commodities that other people want. We depend entirely on keeping in with others. Big shots rely on their power, we nobodies on our connections. With power they can get anything they want; by keeping on good terms with others we can make do. So

---

* One of China's most popular comedians.

don't be so bull-headed. If you haven't learned anything else all these years, you should have learned how
to veer. . . . I know, you needn't explain it to me. The
decision has been announced; still, it can be changed.
Even the Constitution can be changed, and Chairman
Mao made revisions in his writings. You're only a small
factory director. Think you're more infallible than
Chairman Mao and the Constitution? Go on! Get Gong
Ding back. I must make myself clear. It's not the county secretary who sent me here, I came on my own initiative, having your interests at heart. Of course,
Gong Ding did ask me to come and I told him, 'Don't
you worry. Old Ding will do me a little favour like
this.'"

He certainly had the gift of the gab, able to range
from the sublime to the vulgar, to crack jokes or to
scoff.

Originally, Ding Yi had not known that Gong Ding
was a distant relative of the county's first secretary,
and he was not unwilling to reconsider the case. But
all these visitors put him on his guard. If it hadn't
been the first secretary's relative, would so many people have come to urge him to "be prudent", "not to
oversimplify issues" and to "consider the consequences"? This question preoccupied him, to the exclu-
sion of other considerations.

In his annoyance he sent Young Xiao packing.

Two days passed. June 23, Sunday, was a hot, long
mid-summer day. Mosquitoes had kept Ding awake
the previous night, and he had no appetite. At half
past four that morning, a visitor arrived by bus.
He was Ding Yi's brother-in-law. Tall, bespectacled
and bald, he had studied in the Marxist-Leninist Insti-

tute in the 1950s and was now teaching in the prefectural Party school. He was the best-known theorist in the prefecture and enjoyed great prestige. When listening to his lectures, grassroots cadres kept nodding their heads just like chickens pecking millet from the ground. He was the seventeenth visitor in the past two days. As soon as he set foot in the room, he began to talk from a theoretical point of view.

"Socialist society is a transition period in which there exist the scars of capitalism and pre-capitalism. They are inevitable and independent of man's will. This society is superior but not yet mature or perfect. It's only a transition. . . ." After this abstract preamble, he continued:

"So we say, leaders' power, their likes and dislikes, their impressions, are of vital importance. They cannot be overlooked and very often play the decisive role. We are realists, not utopian socialists like Owen and Fourier." (Ding Yi thought: Am I a utopian socialist? This label doesn't sound too bad.) "We are not children or pedants. Our socialism is built on the ground under our feet, which though beautiful, is rather backward and undeveloped." (Ding Yi thought: Have I ever wanted to fly to paradise?) "So when we do any work, we must take all factors into consideration. To use an algebraic formula, there are 'N' factors, not one. The more complicated the world is, the larger the 'N'. . . . So, brother, you were too hasty in handling Gong Ding's case. You didn't use your brain." (Ding Yi thought: A fine brain *you* have, holding forth like this!) "Don't make a gross error, brother. Be statesmanlike. Cancel your decision and invite Gong Ding back."

Ding Yi's wife hastily put in, "That's right, that's right!" A pleased smile appeared on her face. It dawned on Ding Yi that she had asked her theorist brother to talk him round.

While listening, Ding Yi had felt as if his chest was stuffed with hog bristles. His face looked as if he was swallowing a worm. After he had listened attentively for forty minutes, he simply asked, "Did you teach these theories in your Party school?"

Within the twenty-one hours from the arrival of the theorist till 1:45 the next morning, visitors kept coming and going. Some let loose a flood of eloquence, as if they could bring the dying back to life. Some blustered as if they would swallow up the whole world. Some bowed and scraped like swinging willow branches. Some had a well-thought-out plan which they enunciated a word or two at a time, determined not to desist till their goal was reached or, failing that, to hurl Ding Yi over a cliff rather than leave his family in peace. Some brought with them presents ranging from flowers to rancid bean curd. Some promised him a flat with a southern exposure or a brand-new bicycle. Some warned him that he was isolating himself and would come to no good end. Some spoke of the need to protect the Party's prestige — to save the first secretary's face. Some worried about his safety and the fate of his family, some about preserving unity in the country, yet others about human rights, democracy and freedom.

These visitors included Ding Yi's old colleagues, schoolmates, superiors, subordinates, comrades-in-arms, fellow patients in hospital, fellow sufferers, "wine-and-meat" friends and the descendants of his late friends. Some of them were aged people with high prestige, others were promising young ones. Even those who had been in favour of his decision in the factory came over to state that they had changed their minds. Although their motives and manner of speaking differed, they agreed on one point: Gong Ding must not be fired.

Ding Yi had never thought he knew so many people and was known to so many. He could not understand their keen concern for Gong Ding or why his disciplinary action against a contract worker, a hooligan and a distant relative of the county secretary had stirred up such a hornet's nest. He was fast becoming a public enemy! He could neither eat nor rest, nor do any chores. His Sunday was spoilt. He wanted to scream, to smash things, to beat someone up. But instead he gritted his teeth and listened impassively, warning himself, "Keep cool and you'll win through!"

Among the visitors was a star whom Ding Yi had admired when young. Forty years ago, she had been the best-known actress in the province. And Ding Yi in his teens was infatuated for a spell with this woman thirteen years older than himself, although they did not know each other. He had never told anyone of his romantic dream. It was only in the "cultural revolution" when he was undergoing "labour reform" that he had the luck to meet her, an old lady who had retired and now weighed more than eighty kilograms. Due to his oriental, old-fashioned devotion, Ding Yi had always had a special affection for her. To his surprise this "queen" of earlier times also arrived by a donkey cart that day. Sitting on the bed, she prattled through the gaps in her teech:

"I should have come to see you earlier, Young Ding. Look at me, aren't I an old witch? I don't know why

I've aged so suddenly.   Why do so many things come to an end before they've really started? It's like the stage: you're still making up when the music for the final curtain sounds. . . ."

Her lamentation over the transience of life made Ding Yi's eyes moist with tears.   Of all his visitors that day she seemed to him the only one who had called on him out of pure friendship. But what she went on to say took him aback:

"I hear you're a real martinet. That's no way to run a factory. It turns people against you, doesn't it? Do unto others as you would be done by. Haven't you learned anything from your own experience? You'd better not be too hard on young people."

Still, Ding Yi was grateful to her, recalling his youthful dreams. Among the visitors that day, she was the only one who made no mention of Rose-fragrance Paste Factory, Gong Ding and the county secretary.

Some Statistics

I hope readers will excuse me if now I depart from the normal narrative style to publish some correct but well-nigh unbelievable statistics.

In the 12 days from June 21 to July 2, the visitors who came to plead for Gong Ding totalled 199.5 (the former actress didn't mention his name but had him in mind, so she is counted in as 0.5). 33 people telephoned.   27 wrote letters.   53 or 27% really showed keen concern for Ding Yi and were afraid he would run into trouble. 20 or 10% were sent by Gong Ding; 1 or 0.5% by Secretary Li. 63 or 32% were sent by people approached directly or indirectly by Secretary Li. 8 or 4% were asked by Ding Yi's wife to talk round her "die-hard" husband. 46 or 23% were not sent by anyone and did not know Ding Yi but came on their own initiative to do Secretary Li a service. The remaining 4% came for no clear reasons.

Ding Yi refused all his visitors' requests. His stubbornness enraged 85% of them, who immediately spread word that he was a fool. Ding Yi's petty appointment had gone to his head, they claimed, making him stubborn and unreasonable and cutting him off from the masses. They asserted that he was fishing for fame and credit, that he had ulterior motives and was taking this chance to vent his spite because the Party's county committee had not promoted him to a higher position. Some said he was crazy and had always been reactionary, that he should never have been rehabilitated. Assuming that each of them spoke to at least ten people, 1,700 heard talk of this kind. For a while public opinion was strongly against him. It seemed all were out for his blood. His wife fell ill and her life was only saved by emergency measures. Even the nurse in charge of the oxygen cylinder took the chance to ask Ding Yi to change his mind.

Incidents of this kind happen quickly and end quickly too. They are like the breakfast queues in restaurants, which form as soon as fried cakes and porridge are served and disperse immediately after the food is sold out, no matter how angry those balked of fried cakes are. By August there was no further talk of the case, and by September it had escaped people's minds. Meanwhile, the production in the paste factory had gone up each day. By October, great changes had taken place.

When talking together, people stuck up their thumbs saying, "Old Ding Yi really knows a thing or two!"

By December, the fame of the paste factory really had the fragrance of roses.   It had become a model for all the small enterprises in the province.   The Rose-fragrance Paste it produced was consistently of first-rate quality.   Ding Yi went to attend a meeting in the provincial capital at which he was asked to report his experience. He went on to the rostrum, his face flushed, and said, "Communists are made of steel, not paste. . . ."

This caused a general sensation.

He added, "If we don't get down to business, our country's done for!"

He broke off there, choking, and tears ran down his cheeks.

There was a solemn silence for a moment in the auditorium.

Then, thunderous applause!

Translated by Xiong Zhenru

The Butterfly

A jeep made in Beijing was hurtling along a country road. Inside, it was so stuffy that the passenger felt drowsy The motor kept up a roar, now high, now low. A roar of distress or content? People can groan with pleasure. Hadn't Dongdong, nearly four years old in 1956, done just that when taken out to eat ice-cream? To his father he had looked like a kitten that had caught its first mouse, purring contentedly.

The jeep accelerated. Hills flashed past. Before them were villages, cottages and peasants, who automatically lined up to clap. Among them were gaily dressed girls, mischievous boys, who screwed up their eyes to throw pebbles at the jeep, and cheerful, placid grown-ups. There were hayricks higher than the courtyard walls, trees, fields, ponds, roads, hills and hollows, livestock, horsecarts with rubber tires, mini-tractors pulling trailers. . . . Gleaming asphalt and dirt roads half washed away by freshets, as well as the dust and the donkey-dung on them all rushed to meet their jeep, then swept past. The speedometer showed that they were travelling at over sixty kilometres an hour. The spinning wheels kept up an angry, impressive yet indifferent roar. Swishing over the ground they reminded one of skating, rowing, or young people running first thing in the morning. He still went jogging in a blue track suit.

Damn this jeep! Why had it cut him off from the ground, and that clean, fresh air so easily polluted? But travelling this way was comfortable. Besides, it saved precious time. In Beijing, it was considered more dignified to sit in the back. The seat by the driver was left for a secretary, bodyguard or interpreter, who had to be ready to hop out to contact his opposite number while he, the high official, sat stolidly without stirring in the back. Even after the liaison work was completed and his secretary opened the back door and put in his head to report, he remained impassive, as if tired and indifferent. He might even yawn a couple of times. Very often his secretary had to repeat the message before he would nod or shake his head and grunt. This was what was expected of a high official. And it wasn't a put-on show — he was really too busy. Only when in the car did he have a moment to think about himself. So he had learned not to worry about trifles.

Why? His eyes had been closed. Now, suddenly opening, they fell on a small white flower trembling in the middle of the road. What flower was this, still blooming in early winter in a crack in the asphalt road where so much traffic passed? Had he imagined it? By the time he turned to take a closer look, the jeep had run over it. He pictured it crushed. His heart ached as he fancied he heard it sigh. You were crushed like this, weren't you, Haiyun? Love, hate, joy and disillusionment kept you trembling. You were always as transparent, as fragile as a child. But I'm still travelling by jeep.

He sat there quietly next to the driver — in this hilly country that was the custom. Nowadays, wherever he went, he was given the seat of honour. But he wasn't as contented as more than ten years ago. When he left the village that time, Qiuwen and the villagers had gathered round the car to see him off.

"Mind you come back, Old Zhang!" Brother Shuanfu had called, grinning as he tweaked his whiskers.

Shuanfu's wife had wiped away tears and shaded her eyes to watch him affectionately. Not that the sun was dazzling, she just wanted to show how intently she was watching. In Qiuwen's experienced, kindly eyes was a look of expectation he had never seen there before. They had given him a send-off both impressive and light-hearted. For, as Qiuwen said, now they could go their different ways more boldly. Such very different ways! Were they one and the same person, Vice-minister Zhang who rode in a Russian limousine through brightly-lit streets flanked with high-rise buildings, and Old Zhang, a crate of goat-dung on his bowed back, who gritted his teeth to climb the mountain tracks? How had Old Zhang suddenly been transformed into Vice-minister Zhang Siyuan? What was his real identity? This question kept nagging at him.

Qiuwen had urged, "Go and be a good official. We're all for officials like you. We need more of them. . . . If you keep us in your heart, everything will be fine." She had said this slowly, smiling, without a trace of regret. Calmly yet forcefully, like an elder sister comforting a small brother who was crying because he could not fly his kite. Actually she was several years younger than Zhang, now approaching sixty. But today, among his colleagues, a man of sixty counted as "in his prime". Old China! In recent years, old people were expected to soldier on.

When he left that mountain village he felt like a lost soul. He had left Old Zhang there, left Qiuwen and Dongdong. His stone cottage, muck-rake, crate, hoe, straw hat, kerosene lamp, tobacco pouch, millet congee with elm leaves and potatoes . . . he had left them all behind. Qiuwen and Dongdong had lighted up his old age, rejuvenating him. Qiuwen had been the sun in the evening of his life, yet he had left her on the cloud-clad mountain covered with walnut trees. This sun beckoned to him, but he had gone far away. And now, in this jeep, he was rapidly increasing the distance between them.

And Dongdong. Would Dongdong ever understand him? Ever join him? The boy's lack of affection was no more than he deserved on account of Dongdong's mother Haiyun, the trembling little white flower which had been crushed. But he was concerned for Dongdong, still like a ray of light on the horizon, a star which had not yet risen but would surely shed light on him in the end. He was well aware how futile, how harmful it could be for parents to cosset their children and put them in privileged positions. But he secretly wished Dongdong well, for after all he was his only son, even though he would not accept the surname Zhang. He worried about Dongdong's cynicism, although knowing this was natural in young people who had grown up in troubled times and been deceived so often. Of course they were sceptical, bitter. Still, Dongdong had gone too far. He wished his son could understand China's history and real situation, could understand the peasants, the great majority of the population. He didn't want him to go astray, to do anything to harm himself, other people or the country.

The sky cleared. The bright evening sun was rather dazzling. He let down the brown sun-shield and looked out at the gathering dusk. But sunlight dappled his jacket and knees, as from time to time trees cast shadows. He basked in this mottled light with a growing sense of contentment. As the motor roared, the tires swished, and the red and black signs on the dashboard flickered, he was leaving Old Zhang further and further behind, drawing nearer and nearer to the vice-minister.

Busy as he had been, he had asked the minister for a couple of weeks' leave to settle a personal problem — to find himself a wife. That made it sound right and proper. Had he asked to visit two people whom he loved, he would have been accused of "loose living", of turning "revisionist". To describe love as a "problem" and getting married as settling this problem was a distortion of the Chinese language, an insult to human feeling. Yet he used this accepted jargon to ask for leave.

He had left his busy post with a sense of uneasiness. Leaving the comfortable office and flat to which he was accustomed was rather disturbing. But old people, too, have their fancies; and his were choking him. So he slipped away. He travelled on a hard seat by train, then took a long-distance bus, putting up at night in a big doss-house occupied by forty-two people which reeked of tobacco smoke and sweat. Six forty-watt fluorescent lights stayed on all night.

Now he was travelling in a jeep allocated to cadres of his rank. Sitting back on its comfortable seat, he saw in the mirror that he looked clean and alert. Alighting, he put up in a hotel reserved for high-ranking cadres.

It had just had air conditioning installed, and the shower of the gleaming white bath-tub was electrically heated. But all this seemed irrelevant. It was not his choice. He had felt more at home in that far-away mountain village, where he had gone to find Qiuwen, Dongdong and Old Zhang — the happy yet unhappy man whom the villagers trusted.

Now he had left again. After a night in the exclusive hotel and a four hours' flight, he was met at the airport by his secretary and Russian limousine. He realized he was a vice-minister. The bustling streets, with white traffic lines and red lights, were so jammed with people and traffic that they had to wait at every intersection. Two more turns and the car slowed down, then stopped. He shook hands, expressed his thanks, and asked the driver in to rest, but this invitation was declined. His secretary had snatched his few pieces of luggage. In the brightly lit lift the girl attendant with permed hair greeted him. He was back in a place where all who knew his rank would smile at him. He inserted his key in the lock and opened the door himself, not having given the key to his secretary. He didn't want to be waited on all the time. He put on the lights. The walls and floor were spotless as usual, as if polished every day. He was back. He sat down on a sofa.

Haiyun

It seemed to have happened only yesterday. Haiyun's voice was still ringing faintly in his ears, still floating in the air. Although muted, it still could be heard. And her slender figure, shedding radiance around her, where had it fled? Was she really dead? Or still to be seen in some remote part of the universe? The light emitted this instant from some star of a different system would not be visible on earth for centuries. So might not her radiance live on after she had gone?

But no, those happenings belonged to the past, to a bygone generation. He must be in his dotage, dwelling on the events of so many decades ago. Perhaps a hundred or five hundred years from now, Haiyun and others like her would still be remembered. Perhaps his memories, sweet, bitter and ardent, would live on in the mind of some youngster in a happy, just society (by no means a paradise) hundreds of years from now.

Was it in an earlier life that he had met Haiyun? In 1949, singing revolutionary songs they had liberated China. The war years had been hard with their marches, withdrawals, temporary setbacks, casualties, bloodshed and hunger. Sometimes, in disguise they had infiltrated a KMT-occupied city, where the enemy was on the alert for "Reds". Counting their own lives as nothing, the people's army, led by the Communist Party, had advanced to victory. And each time their armed forces entered a city, they danced the folk dances of Yan'an and beat waist-drums. Dancing with red silk they had liberated the whole mainland. They thought they were ushering in a golden age of justice, morality and prosperity.

He was twenty-nine that year, with a black moustache, dressed in a grey cadre's outfit. His armband bore the inscription "Municipal Military Commission of the Chinese People's Liberation Army". He felt and behaved like a triumphant Prometheus bringing happiness and freedom to mankind. He could work as many as twenty hours a day without even feeling tired. Set on transforming the world, he felt stronger than other young people, more experienced than the old ones, because as a "veteran" revolutionary he was a man in a thousand. He was vice-chairman of the military commission of this city. Every day he received the heads of underground Party organizations, leaders of the garrison troops, trade unions and student associations, as well as technicians, capitalists and KMT officers who had come over. He expounded ideas which were utterly new to most of them, couched in new terminology. Personifying the Party, the revolution and victory, he had enormous prestige. His every word was carefully listened to, noted down and studied. His instructions went into immediate effect. "We must change the old currency and stabilize prices." The currency was changed, prices were stabilized. "We must have social order." Hooligans and thieves disappeared; there were no more burglaries, lost goods were returned. "We must end opium-smoking and prostitution." No sooner said than done. His word was law.

One day he was addressing the municipal committee when in came a slender girl in a snowy white blouse. Looking back on it now, she was little more than a child.

How old was she then? Sixteen. Thirteen years younger than he was. Frail with glowing, trustful, spirited eyes. When she spoke to him she fixed her big eyes on him because, to her, he was the Party. A student in a missionary school, she was chairman of the students' self-governing body. Because her classmates had taken part in the celebrations to welcome the PLA, they had clashed with the school authorities and foreign nuns. Haiyun got quite carried away as she described what had happened. When later the students triumphed, she came back.

"All the students hope you'll go and give them a talk," she said. "About the significance of our victory."

"All the students? What about you?" he asked casually.

But this girl's intrusion brightened up his office, as a white dove makes the clear sky seem even bluer. She had made an impression on him.

"Me? That goes without saying. I'd like to listen to you every day."

Did she say that because she loved him? Of course it was the Party that she loved. He and she went to her school in a clattering tram. For in those days there were fewer cars and he didn't insist on going out in one — it wasn't yet a status symbol. As there were no empty seats they were strap-hangers. And Haiyun talked all the way.

"Two KMT spies in our form are in a panic. They spread rumours that Chiang Kai-shek's bombers had razed Shanghai to the ground. We held a struggle meeting against them, and because of this four girls applied to join the Youth League. . . . We had a discussion on the communist philosophy of life. . . ."

When he entered the auditorium the girls clapped enthusiastically. Their eyes sparkled with respect and tears of joy. The microphone had broken down. It took half an hour to have it fixed. Haiyun went up to the platform to conduct the girls in singing revolutionary songs. She did this with great competence and gusto.

> The People's Government loves the people,
> The goodness of the Party
> Is beyond words. . . .

The hall rang with the singing of these enthusiastic girls. Haiyun, conducting, seemed the incarnation of spring. When the microphone was repaired he gave his talk.

"Youth Leaguers!" Applause. "Students, greetings! I give you a revolutionary salute!" Applause. "You are the masters of the new society, the new life. Your predecessors shed their blood to open up a bright, broad road for you. You must advance from victory to victory." Heads bent, murmuring agreement, the girls were taking down every word, but they still punctuated his speech with clapping. "A new chapter has started in the history of China and mankind. We are no longer slaves, the victims of fate. We no longer need sigh or weep. With our own hands we are going to build up our future, seize back all that was lost, create all that we never had. After wiping out oppression and all that is selfish and backward, we shall have lost only our chains, but won the world. . . ." Redoubled applause. He saw tears of exaltation in Haiyun's eyes and on the eyelashes of the other girls. Through these tears they saw red flags, a lighthouse, bugles, hydro-electric stations. . . . How could he have spoken so fervidly? Much of it was empty, childish talk. But he believed in it, and so did his audience. The past had been burned to ashes in the flames of revolution. Now their prospects were brilliant. Their new life was in their own hands. . . .

Later he and Haiyun corresponded, telephoned, met,

strolled in the parks, went to films or ate ice-cream together. Most of their time, however, was spent on political instruction. He seemed omniscient, able to answer all her questions about the world, China, life, the Party's history, the Soviet Union or the work of the Youth League. Haiyun would watch him devotedly, earnestly. When, unable to control himself, he took her in his arms and kissed her, she did not resist him and gave no sign of shyness. She worshipped him and would do whatever he wanted. And wasn't she equally dear to him? Hadn't it been a case of love at first sight? All his colleagues' warnings to him fell on deaf ears. Haiyun's parents' opposition was equally useless. They got married when he was thirty-one, she eighteen. Haiyun left school without waiting to graduate, and became a typist in a Party committee office.

In 1950 their first child was born. Just at the time when the Chinese People's Volunteers went to Korea, and a counter-revolutionary plot was discovered in this city. For over a month he was so busy organizing supplies for the Volunteers, doing propaganda work and dealing with counter-revolutionaries that he could not go home, only three kilometres away from his office. One day, during an important meeting, Haiyun phoned. The baby had a high fever, she was afraid. . . .

"I'm busy," he said and rang off, rather ashamed as he imagined her sobbing. He decided to go home after the meeting. But most cadres were then too busy to go home at night, not even at the weekends or New Year. It was for the revolution! Each extra moment they worked would speed up the victory of the world revolution, bring sunshine so much the sooner to end the sufferings of the Korean people. It was 1:40 a.m. when the meeting ended. But when he got home. . . .

Their child, their first son, was dead.

Haiyun seemed in a trance. She stared blankly at her husband and simply looked dazed when he questioned her and tried to comfort her. Blaming himself, he broke down and fell on his knees in front of the dead child and the young mother. Still she remained stupefied.

"You mustn't just think of yourself, Haiyun!" he cried. "We aren't ordinary people. We're Party members, Bolsheviks. This very second, American planes are bombing Pyongyang, thousands of Korean children are being killed by napalm. . . ." Carried away, he lectured her regardless of her feelings as a mother. Then, summoned by his bodyguard, he hurried away.

That was the start of their estrangement. Haiyun was a petty-bourgeois intellectual who had not been re-moulded and lacked experience. Such people often tend to vacillate. In addition, she paid too much attention to trifles. And to her he may have appeared increasingly callous, selfish and arrogant. Because he blamed himself for disrupting her education and destroying her happiness, he succeeded in getting her into a good university in Shanghai to study foreign literature — the subject she liked best. At the station, when the whistle went and the train was about to pull out, Haiyun, dressed like a student, leaned out of the window to wave. Her face was radiant. It seemed she had never been in love or married, never had a child and lost him; she was still the chairman of the students' union in that missionary school, now going to college in Shanghai to conduct the singing of revolutionary songs. And he was still a young "veteran" revolutionary, a leading cadre who forgot himself in his work. Their relationship was still so simple and pure.

Absence makes the heart grow fonder. They corresponded. He missed Haiyun very much. But those were stirring times. He led the movement to oppose corruption, and they exposed fourteen scoundrels who had embezzled huge sums of public money (although later investigations proved that only two of them were really guilty). He revelled in this success. Then came the movement to root out counter-revolutionaries. They studied the documents about Hu Feng's "counter-revolutionary clique" and another witch-hunt began. Guns and transmitters were discovered, counter-revolutionaries were ferreted out, and many suspects were investigated. One movement followed another, to weed out the scum of the old society.

In '56, he was appointed secretary of the municipal Party committee. Every move he made, every word he said influenced the city's three hundred thousand people. They watched his every action. He was the brain, the policy-maker there, who supervised all the work from wiping out flies to setting up factories, and saw that it was well done. Considering himself a part of a vast machine imbued him with vision, energy and a sense of responsibility. This gave his life its meaning.

But his relations with Haiyun failed to improve. When she came back from Shanghai for the winter vacation, their love for each other revived. They talked about Flaubert and Maupassant. However, he knew no more about French literature than she did about the work of the Party committee, and the questions he asked set her laughing. Haiyun realized that, to please her, he didn't mind exposing his ignorance; so in return she took an interest in the municipal elections and the budget. Once they cooked a fish together, and he discovered that she surpassed the best chefs in the restaurants; but she wouldn't tell him what ingredients she used. When New Year and the Lantern Festival had passed and she had to leave, an important meeting stopped him from seeing her off. Then Haiyun wrote to say she was pregnant again. He urged her to have an abortion. This so enraged her that he received no more letters for four months. When the summer vacation came she returned, big with child.

"We've already lost one son," she said, eyeing him resentfully.

Conscience-stricken, after the child was born he not only engaged a well-trained nurse but got the best doctor in the new children's hospital to call in regularly. Haiyun had asked for six months' leave, but she extended this to a year, unwilling to leave her second, now only son. Zhang felt she might as well give up her studies, because whether she graduated or not she could be sure of respect and a good job. But Haiyun insisted on finishing her course in Shanghai. The evening before she left she wept over little Dongdong, then nearly one. . . .

There are storms in nature, clashes among men. Life is so full of contradictions! The moon wanes then waxes again. How can you be certain that tonight's full moon is the same as that pale crescent of two weeks ago? Rivers flow, wave after wave, but where is the difference, the connection between them?

Haiyun, Haiyun, did we understand each other? Why couldn't you forgive me?

Rumours started spreading, some well-meant, some

malicious. Couldn't a man in charge of a large city keep his own wife under control? He groaned inwardly. . . . Why was it then that when Haiyun returned, wearing her old student clothes in preference to the smarter ones he had bought her, he felt completely at a loss, quite unable to reproach her.

"For the sake of our child. . . ." he pleaded.

Haiyun said nothing, but wept. She left college, and promised to break with her lover there. Although she had not graduated, she became an instructor in the local normal college, and soon was appointed assistant secretary of her Party branch. That set Zhang's mind at rest.

Then — a bolt from the blue — in '57 Haiyun was labelled a Rightist.

"How could you degenerate like this — praising anti-Party novels? Who are you? And who am I? Had you forgotten?" Hands behind his back, he paced up and down, adamant, ruthless. "You must admit your fault and turn over a new leaf."

Each word he said made Haiyun flinch. Then she raised her head and he was appalled by the icy look in her eyes. . . .

A month later Haiyun asked for a divorce. He still wanted to save their marriage, but it was clear that they would have to split up. The last time he saw her, after their divorce, he was furious to see that her face was radiant.

"She really has degenerated," he told himself.

Every spring the fresh leaves on the trees are full of life as they drink in the rain and sunshine or greet the warbling birds. They enliven the courtyards, roads and countryside and seem to be blessing young lovers. They are waiting for the luxuriance of summer, willing to wither in autumn and finally to be blown down without regret. Because they have lived, grown, loved. Though only little leaves, they have done all they can for their parent tree, for birds and for lovers. But what if a leaf is destroyed in spring or at the start of summer? Wouldn't that fill it with regret? Although a tree has thousands of leaves, and next year will put out thousands more, and although the tree will not die in the foreseeable future, that particular leaf will never come back to life, never drink in the sunshine or spring rain again.

But cars were speeding ahead at sixty kilometres an hour, trains at a hundred, aircraft at nine hundred, while satellites hurtled through space at twenty-eight thousand.

Meilan

Meilan was a strange mixture of contradictions: slippery as a fish, downy as a white swan, tenacious as pliers.

As soon as Haiyun left, Meilan arrived. Maybe this was contrived by colleagues concerned for him. They had never approved of their municipal secretary having a wife like a schoolgirl. Meilan, lustrous and fragrant, with a face like a full moon, was determined to fill the gap left by Haiyun and fully confident that she could do so. When lost in thought, her face was inscrutable and two rather sinister furrows appeared on her forehead. But these disappeared as soon as she saw Zhang Siyuan, and she smiled bewitchingly. Her coming transformed his life. His whole standard of living suddenly improved. "It's for your work," she would reason. The old sofa was replaced by a new one covered with gold brocade, where he could relax in comfort. He had the impression that she was always asking the administration office for this or that.

"Don't make so many requests," he protested. "We don't want to live in such style. That old sofa was quite good enough. Why have it changed?"

"Just look at you!" Meilan laughed. "You're old before your time from overwork and hardly ever come home to rest, so you deserve a few comforts."

He said nothing. His whole mind was on smelting steel. For that was the time when many families smashed their cooking pans for scrap-iron.* The anti-Rightist campaign, the movements to combat rightist trends and conservatism had kept him under a strain. It was a long time since he had relaxed. A soft new glossy sofa, just like an attentive, smart new wife, was not such a luxury. Only sometimes he was disturbed by the suspicion that his life was being run by Meilan — she was leading him by the nose. And occasionally he had a mental picture of Haiyun, short, slim and unsophisticated. But when he opened his eyes she had gone, like a sapling glimpsed from the window of a train, then rapidly left behind. He had no time to miss her.

His Downfall

What is the relation between men and their surroundings?

Secretary Zhang, ensconced in his brocade sofa, smok-

---

*In 1958 during the Big Leap Forward movement, there was a call to speed up the production of steel.

ing the best filter-tipped cigarettes and spinning out his words as he addressed those gathered round to take notes, was obsequiously treated by all. No matter where he was or what he was doing, he was singled out for respect. What difference was there between him and that Eighth Route Army cultural instructor in puttees, or that political commissar Zhang Siyuan who had crawled through the undergrowth for two days and nights to escape the enemy? Weren't they the same man? Hadn't the aim of that hard struggle been to win political power and reform China? Whether sleeping in the undergrowth, on a peasant's heated *kang* or on a spring-bed, hadn't he given all his strength and time to the great cause of the Party? He had never forgotten those hard years or his revolutionary ideals. Petty-bourgeois anarchy, or that type of "revolutionary" who equated death with victory had no place in China. Had he changed? If not, why was he so afraid of losing his sofa, spring-bed and limousine? Could he still sleep as soundly now on a *kang*?

In self-justification he told himself it wasn't just for comfort that he was afraid of losing his leading position. He was afraid of losing his fighting post, his important postion in the great Communist Party. These years he had led many movements, had seen the wretchedness of those ousted from power. It was a fearful thing to be dragged out and condemned, and the condemnation was irrevocable. As municipal secretary he considered himself in charge of the whole city, yet when Haiyun was labelled a Rightist he was completely helpless. And he himself had condemned many other people. Overnight a smug leading cadre became spurned by everyone, treated like dirt. He had to abase himself and hang his head. It was as magical as a beautiful princess transformed into a toad, or a mighty king into a leprous beggar.

He had never dreamed that this could happen to him. During every movement he proclaimed, "In struggle the proletariat knows the joy of victory. We revel in it. Only those classes doomed to die out dread the class struggle." Why then had he been dismayed in '66 by the drums and gongs of the Red Guards?

Later on he often looked back on how it had happened. At the start of the Cultural Revolution, he had felt both elated and tense. He saw this as a ruthless but great and inspiring movement. However, its violence took him by surprise. Well, he was not afraid of storms, he would meet the wind and waves head on. He believed this struggle was to combat revisionism, to revolutionize China. He knew that many more leading cadres would be toppled, but for the Party's sake he must not be soft-hearted. He sanctioned the criticism of the newspaper editor, which was a violent political attack. Then the local chairman of the Federation of Literary and Art Circles was denounced. The papers kept issuing warnings to beware of capitalist-roaders who victimized subordinates to save their own skin. So to find a more highly placed scapegoat, he hardened his heart and denounced the head of the municipal propaganda department. And then the vice-secretary in charge of education. As more and more cadres were overthrown, he himself became more exposed and vulnerable. And finally his turn came.

Even so it took him by surprise. It seemed unthinkable that he should be cursed and spat at, called a capitalist-roader and renegade. This was surely not the same Zhang Siyuan who had sat in the municipal office with guards at its gate. There were two rooms to his office. The outer, larger one, had a slightly worn carpet and various charts on the wall. In it were a desk with a telephone and a sofa. That was where his secretary sat, working conscientiously. The inner room, his sanctum, had handsome lamps, a brand-new carpet, a big black hardwood desk, a leather revolving chair and a comfortable bed for his siesta. Here he read documents, wrote comments, made telephone calls, thought over problems, then instructed his secretary to carry out his decisions. By rights, a Party secretary of a city should not have had a private secretary, but he had been assigned one. He concentrated on the work of the municipality and had no time to attend to his private affairs. For seventeen years he had taken no holiday. Even when he watched local operas which he had loved since his childhood, he would often be interrupted by urgent messages or telephone calls. He lived solely for his work, and did not believe the city could do without him.

But now a different Zhang Siyuan had emerged, who bowed his head and confessed to his crimes, unable to defend himself when beaten, abused, slandered, tortured. Nobody sympathized with him. He was not allowed to rest or go home, to have a haircut or bath, to wear anything but cotton or to smoke good cigarettes. He was a criminal, a homeless cur ostracized by the Party and the people.

Is this me? Is Zhang Siyuan a counter-revolutionary? Only two weeks ago I was running this city. Is this broken Zhang Siyuan me? Am I really wearing this padded cotton jacket smeared with paste? (Red Guards had stuck a big-character poster on his back, then emptied a bucket of paste down his neck). Is this old dodderer, watched even when he goes to the lavatory, the tall, vigorous, confident Secretary Zhang? This hoarse throat, is it the Party secretary's which issued such ringing, resolute instructions?

Time and again he puzzled over this question. He reached the conclusion: This must be a nightmare. A mistake. A cruel joke. It was inconceivable that he should be treated as an enemy of the Party and the people. This "counter-revolutionary" Zhang Siyuan, a mangy cur who wished he were dead, was a ridiculous travesty of himself. A big-character poster said: The Red Guards have exposed Zhang Siyuan's true features. No! This was a travesty. He must stick it out, stand this test.

But when Dongdong boxed his ears that undermined his morale.

Dongdong

A father's feeling for his child is not the same as a mother's who from the start is much closer to her baby. Zhang Siyuan felt no such close ties to this tiny, howling creature. But because their first son had died, when Dongdong was born in the winter of '52 he adopted a most protective attitude towards him. It stemmed from a sense of responsibility and was not really love. Haiyun was the one he loved and, knowing how she doted on this baby son, during her confinement he made a show of being devoted to Dongdong.

Ten months later Haiyun had to go back to college.

By then Dongdong could stand up and take a few steps, leaning against the wall. He could call "Uncle". To Zhang's annoyance, his son always called him "Uncle". He had eight teeth and could eat biscuits. In fact once, his eyes watering, he finished off a whole onion. All this made him seem more of an individual, a new person in Zhang Siyuan's life who would be a companion for him. This thought warmed his father's heart. Sometimes, snatching a moment from work, he would telephone home to ask how Dongdong was.

After this came word that Haiyun was having an affair with one of her classmates. Through his mind flashed the base suspicion: Is Dongdong really mine? To hell with it! I've no time to waste worrying about this. I'm responsible for the fate of three hundred thousand people. He was too busy to spare any time for Dongdong.

However, he forgave Haiyun, because he was broad-minded and he loved her. He couldn't bear to see tears on her childlike face. But what if his love was the cause of her unhappiness, of her tears like spring rain?

In the spring of '54, going home through the rain, he saw Dongdong's face pressed against the window-pane, his little nose flattened and white. Spring rain! Dongdong was staring unblinkingly at this miraculous phenomenon. It was the first time in his life he had watched the rain. His father, so occupied with meetings and documents, felt touched and stirred. Spring, green leaves and rain — they existed for the young. Only children could grasp their beauty and enchantment. He did not disturb his son. His own dear son! He went off eager to shoulder heavy burdens for tens of thousands of children, to devote all his strength to the greatest cause of mankind. Dongdong should have a much better life than his father's generation. How he wished him happiness!

After that, he spent all his spare time with his son, convinced that Dongdong would grow up like himself, When he lifted him on to a chair in the milk bar, they sat there like equals to enjoy a cold drink and when his son purred with pleasure over an ice-cream, he shared in his delight. When Dongdong had finished he lifted him up and held him high over his head. See, my son is taller than I am! His love for Dongdong was a masculine love, based less on consanguinity than on friendship.

But this friendship of theirs was wrecked by the boy's mother. In '57, Haiyun in one of her classes praised some stories attacking the Party on the pretext of opposing bureaucracy. Zhang didn't read these stories till twenty years later. Why didn't I read them earlier, he wondered? Well, even if I'd had the time it would have been no use, because in those days our convictions triumphed over truth and reason. So Haiyun became an anti-Party Rightist opposed to socialism, an agent of the imperialists, a wolf in sheep's clothing, a poisonous snake disguised as a beautiful woman, far more dangerous and treacherous than Chiang Kai-shek. As a result, naturally, she asked for a divorce. He did his best to dissuade her, but to no purpose. After their divorce he kept telling himself that he was not to blame, but that made him feel rather a hypocrite, like someone singing in the dark to keep up his courage.

What about Dongdong? They didn't discuss him much. "I shall still be his father, you will still be his mother" — that went without saying. To begin with,

Dongdong lived with him; later on, with his mother. When his father had time, he sent a car to fetch him. But Dongdong was very precocious. He no longer considered ice-creams or sundaes a treat.

Later on Meilan took up all Zhang Siyuan's free time, though they had no child of their own. And he enjoyed the comfortable, orderly life that she arranged for him. Meilan valued orderliness more than happiness. In the morning he drank tea, in the evening spirits. In the morning he washed his face in tepid water, in the evening he had a hot bath. When they went by car to see a film, she would send the driver to buy fresh bamboo shoots. She ran everything like clockwork. But all she brought him was comfort, a monotonous sense of well-being which made him feel satiated, it was so insipid. Several times he sent for Dongdong, but the boy had gone to school. So one day in '64 he drove to the primary school in the suburbs to see him. He didn't want to see Haiyun. Especially since she had married that college classmate of hers. He felt that her remarriage was a tribute to his integrity. It cleared his conscience.

Dongdong in '64 was thin and pale, obviously undernourished. In '60, at the start of the hard years, his father had often sent him expensive cream cakes and chocolates, but these hadn't made him strong. In fact, Zhang Siyuan suspected that these gifts had estranged his son. When he saw him now in '64, Dongdong emphasized how good his dad was to him. He now called his step-father dad and Zhang Siyuan father, and addressed him ceremoniously though only twelve. His respectful, wary attitude reminded Zhang of his subordinates. And when Meilan learned that he had been to see Dongdong, she put wordless pressure on him: those two furrows in her forehead reappeared, and her forced, unnatural laughter sent a shiver down his spine. So he stopped visiting Dongdong. For the Spring Festival of '65, he sent some cakes to the boy's school. They were returned untouched with the following note:

> Thank you, father. Please don't take offence, but don't send me any more cakes.

That did offend him! All his subordinates treated him with respect. He could lose his temper with them with impunity. Besides, a show of temper was an indispensable part of his power. Yet here was Dongdong treating him like this. Ridiculous!

When he grows up he'll understand, Zhang thought. He'll seek me out. He'll realize what an asset it is to have an old revolutionary, a municipal secretary as his father.

Two years later he was standing with bowed head on the platform being denounced. "Down with the renegade and spy Zhang Siyuan! Zhang Siyuan must come clean! Smash Zhang Siyuan's head! Diehard . . . dog-shit. . . ." The bedlam was deafening. His hair painfully tugged, he was forced to bend almost double. But all this would pass, he had been through it before.

Then a youngster bounded up. Zhang glanced at him. Heavens! Dongdong. He boxed Zhang on the left ear with all his might, as if he wanted to kill him. Excruciating pain, like an electric shock, nearly made him throw up. Then Dongdong slapped his right ear. By the time the third blow landed Zhang had passed out.

When he came to he heard a youngster screaming at him — yes, it was Dongdong.

Class revenge! This could only be explained in terms of class struggle. Haiyun was already condemned as a class enemy. But although the masses were investigating him, he was still the Party secretary of the city, appointed with the approval of the Central Committee. The revolutionary masses, out for his blood, had accused him of many crimes; but no verdict had yet been passed. So his case was totally different from Haiyun's. They belonged to different classes.

Maybe Dongdong, taking his mother's reactionary stand, had been told by her to kill his father. Surely "only Left-wingers can rebel, not Rightists". But in this unprecedented Great Proletarian Cultural Revoution, bad elements were bound to mix with the good, and all sorts of opportunists would come to the fore. Evidently Dongdong was one. Some time he must alert the revolutionaries guarding him to this problem, this new trend in the class struggle. They must crack down on people who really loathed the Party and socialism.

But he himself cracked up first. A few days later he heard that Haiyun had hanged herself. Shortly after, he learned that Meilan had written a poster completely dissociating herself from him. But this second piece of news affected him not at all.

A Judgement

I ask to be tried.

You are innocent.

No. That tram's clattering is a dirge for Haiyun. The day that she came to my office to see me, her fate was sealed.

She sought you out. She loved you. You gave her happiness.

I ruined her. I neglected our first son, I can't even remember his features. I wounded Dongdong, I understand that now. The chocolate and cakes I sent him must have shown him the gulf between me and his dearly loved mother. When she shed tears I should have wiped them away. Instead I read her a lecture. If not for me, she could have studied happily at college and after graduation found a husband more suited to her. Because of me that was impossible. I made her so wretched that, in '57, she criticized the Party.

But you loved her, didn't you?

Everyone has to die. If only, before leaving this world, I could tell her: Haiyun, I love you! But if I really loved her I shouldn't have married her. We don't believe in spirits. Supposing, though, we were to be reincarnated, I'd gladly fall at her feet to beg her to sentence me, to punish me.

You're human, your status doesn't deprive you of the right to love, to respond to a girl's love.

But I, being more mature, should have shown more sense of responsibility. I shouldn't have thrust myself on such an innocent young girl.

In 1949, weren't you innocent and young? That was the childhood of our People's Republic, the childhood of us all.

But why didn't I try to protect her? I should have stayed with her, whatever the cost.

Later on she stopped loving you, she was too fickle. She had a lover at college. She was the one to blame.

What makes me wretched is this — there's no one to punish me.

There is.
Who?
Dongdong.

The Mountain Village

The ancient philosopher Zhuangzi dreamed that he turned into a butterfly flitting this way and that. He awoke to a problem of identity. Was he Zhuangzi, awake, or a butterfly having a dream?

This whimsical story rather saddened Zhang. For now in *his* dream, he had changed not into a butterfly but a criminal, an outcast, denied a trial, unable to live but without the right to die. This prison was one he had had built when in power to imprison class enemies. . . .

But he awoke at last from this stifling dream. In '70 he was released, for no apparent reason, just as three years ago he had suddenly been imprisoned. And now he had no family, for during his confinement Meilan had divorced him, taking away all their family possessions. To him this was welcome news.

He was a butterfly again. "Your case isn't being considered yet," he was told. An Eighth Route Army cadre from a mountain gully had turned into a high official, then a target for the revolutionary masses, then a prisoner in solitary confinement, and now a butterfly, all on his own. They were hard to take, all these changes!

Unlike some overthrown cadres, he did not just hope to have his case declared "a contradiction within the ranks of the people". For an old Party member, a municipal secretary, that would have been ludicrous. He needed to live on, reflect, and find his son.

So in the spring of '71 he went to the distant village where Dongdong was working. The foot of the mountain was a riot of apricot blossom. Brooks spilled down winding valleys, throwing up silver spray. The whole place teemed with life. Under the thin ice on the northern slope, fish were swimming in flowing water. The southern slope was a vivid green — the grass had survived the winter. Mischievous squirrels jumped from tree to tree. On the rocks below were scattered the apricot stones they had cracked. Grass snakes slithered through the dead leaves. Hares ran like the wind. . . .

The mountain paths were twisting, and yet less tortuous than men's way through life. But no matter how many troubles beset the country, spring had returned again. He really longed to become a butterfly, to flit over the snowy heights to the valleys where brooks gurgled through dense forests to terraced fields. Some youngsters were ploughing the fields. The one in front, his black padded jacket slung over his shoulders, suddenly burst into song:

> Tell me, sister, who did you wrong?
> Don't take it so hard,
> Don't drown yourself. . . .

Haiyun hadn't drowned herself but put her head in a noose. Zhang Siyuan had felt the constriction round her throat the second after she kicked the stool away and the rope tightened, strangling her. The thought of it robbed him of speech. His vocal chords had been injured. It was on this pretext that he had asked not to go to the cadres' school but instead to the village where his son was working.

He had come here as a "common citizen" with no official title, no authority, and no reputation either good or bad. Just as he had come into the world some fifty years ago. As soon as he arrived, his son had himself transferred to another village. Well, mutual understanding would come with time. He settled down quietly, in no hurry to get to know his son. He must first know himself.

Up in the mountains he discovered his legs, which he had ignored for years. Helping the peasants winnow or fetch water, he discovered his arms, his shoulders. Straightening up from hoeing to watch a jeep raising a cloud of dust on the road, he discovered his eyes. In the past, he had sat in comfort in a jeep looking out through the windscreen at the peasants working.

He discovered that he still held attraction for women. Why otherwise were those peasant women so eager to chat and joke with him? The horseplay and crude speech of the married people here shocked him, but he could condone it. Why shouldn't they have a bit of fun during a work break? They had so little pleasure in their lives. You couldn't expect them to use their breaks reciting Chairman Mao's works. They wanted the earth to yield better crops, not to soar above the clouds. He Zhang Siyuan, was the one who had soared, airborne, through the clouds.

Here, too, he discovered his own intelligence, his ideal, his self respect. For seventeen years he had been respected by all. But overnight that respect had become contempt, savagery, abuse. Even Meilan and his son had left him. Evidently it had not been Zhang Siyuan whom they respected, but the municipal secretary. With his position he lost everything else. Now things had changed: the peasants sympathized with him and trusted him. They took him their problems because he was a decent fellow with good sense, concerned for others.

But this made no impact on Dongdong. The first time Zhang went to see him, his son was laboriously mending a shoe with an awl and thick needle, a very amateur cobbler.

"Why don't you say anything?" his father asked.

"What is there to say? Why did you have to come here? I've changed my surname, don't call myself Zhang any more."

"That's up to you. Still, there are only the two of us left. We have no other folks."

"If you get reinstated, I suppose you'll start by killing a whole lot of people. Vice-commander Lin Biao has taught us: political power is the power of suppression. Wouldn't I be your first victim?"

"Don't talk such nonsense."

"Why not admit that you hate me? You recognized me, didn't you, that day I beat you? What did you think? Class struggle, class revenge . . . eh?"

Zhang Siyuan shuddered.

"That's better. Let's be honest. I prefer honest hate to sham love." In his agitation Dongdong jabbed the thumb of his left hand with his needle. He started sucking it, the image of his mother when she had pricked a finger while sewing on a button.

"Will you tell me something about your mother's last days?"

"I don't know anything."

"Impossible."

"After I beat you that day, I was hauled off by the

police. Only Left-wingers not Rightists, can revolt. That was your slogan, remember?"

Shuddering, Zhang croaked as he felt the rope choking him.

"What's wrong with you?"

Dongdong helped him on to his bed, then poured him a cup of water.

"Why ... do you ... avoid me?" Zhang wheezed.

For a while Dongdong made no answer. Then he asked, "Can you forgive me?"

"Maybe I'm the one who should be asking forgiveness."

"Do you know why I beat you?"

"For your mother. . . ."

"No!" Dongdong broke in. "I beat you, really and truly, as a revolutionary rebel. The head of our contingent put me up to it. In fact, after you were denounced, mother often told me it was a lot of slander. . . . It may have been partly because I didn't listen to her that she killed herself. Of course, the main reason was those fearful beatings. She couldn't take it. I. . . ."

Tears coursed down his cheeks. Zhang's heart ached. They were reconciled.

However, after Zhang had established a closer relationship with his son, he came across his diary. It was cynical, decadent. Dongdong had written, "I've had enough of these swindlers' lies, hypocrisy and highfalutin talk.... People are utterly selfish.... Life's hell on earth." As he read on, Zhang's hands trembled. Was it for this that our generation battled, shed blood and slaved away day and night? For you, who have had it

so easy, to moan in this despicable way? He and Dongdong had a heated argument.

"Stand?" demanded Dongdong. "What do you think
my stand is? Of course, *you* people take the stand
of the Party. You made sacrifices, hum? But
what you've got from the Party is more than you
gave to it! Even when you were in prison, your monthly
salary was more than a peasant earns in a whole year.
Besides, you could be sure that sooner or later you'd
be re-enthroned as municipal secretary!"

"Shut up!" snapped Zhang Siyuan. "You can swear
at me, but don't you slander our Party! Don't slander
our whole generation of revolutionaries. Li Dazhao,
Fang Zhimin . . . they gave their lives for the people.
. . ."

"So that we should drag on like this?"

"That's dangerous talk — it's too reactionary!"

"Want to put me in prison? You didn't build that
prison for yourselves, did you?"

Zhang Siyuan could not speak for fury. Had he heard
such talk five years ago, no matter from whom, he
would have arrested the speaker. Cursing under his
breath he flung off.

On his way back to his lodgings a storm broke. Lightning flashed through the tree-tops, thunder cracked
overhead. Rain poured down. The mountain track
seemed a brook, his shoes were sopping. The storm
suited his mood. He longed to be struck by lightning!

He slipped and fell.

Rehabilitation

I wonder why
Every day I sigh,

And pray to heaven above
To free me from the loneliness of love. . . .

This Hong Kong pop song had caught on all over the country. When first he heard that youngsters were recording Hong Kong music, he simply smiled disdainfully. He had never had any respect for Hong Kong culture. When travelling incognito back to the place where for six years he had worked as Old Zhang, he put up for the night in a hostel for ordinary cadres before changing to another bus the next day. A buyer for a trade corporation in the same room played this song on his tape-recorder, over and over.

Zhang Siyuan was no musician. He had learned to read musical scores and beat time while in the army. All the Eighth Route Army soldiers loved to sing. This was the first thing that struck new arrivals to the liberated areas. One song started:

Clear the sky over the liberated area
And happy the people there;
The sun there never sets,
No end to the singing. . . .

By comparing such songs with the decadent ones of KMT-occupied areas, you could tell to whom the future of China belonged.

But what was happening now? After thirty years of education, of singing *Socialism Is Good* and other revolutionary songs, the whole country was being swept by "the loneliness of love"!

Tempted to smash the tape-recorder, he paced the floor, clenching his fists. How utterly bogus! Utterly frivolous! What did they know about love, those young people dancing in discotheques, smoking cigarettes and sipping champagne while flirting? Any talk of the West, of Hong Kong or even of Taiwan set their mouths watering. Instead of studying, sweating, working at night they spent their time dreaming about refrigerators, streamlined furniture and spring-beds. Such cheap posturing — it made him want to vomit.

A mawkish, vulgar song, sung by a second-rate singer. Yet it was sweeping the country. Even if banned — would we do such a stupid thing again? Who knows? It would still be all the rage.

The song had a soporific effect. But Vice-minister Zhang couldn't sleep. Since his rehabilitation in April '75 he hadn't had a single good night's sleep.

In April '75 he'd been living with his son in a small cottage in the mountains. For some time, thanks to Dr Qiuwen's good offices, he'd been reconciled with Dongdong. He was making dumplings with fresh, green leeks. When Dongdong came back they might invite Qiuwen and her daughter to share them. After a winter of eating turnips and cabbage, fresh green leeks, even if soiled with donkey-dung, seemed to bring spring into their cottage. These leeks were inextricably bound up with the warmth they hadn't experienced for months, caroling birds, tricklets of melted snow, clear lengthening days, the vitality pulsing in Nature, and the subtle strength of love. Even hearts scarred with grief felt a fresh stir of hope. This was doubly true of Zhang Si-yuan after a childhood of poverty and oppression, a youth dyed red with blood. The Party had shown him the way to take; the people's respect and trust had impelled him forward. And this spring he sensed that a change was in the air. Things could not go on like this.

How could the Party be unclear about questions of right and wrong which were clear even to children? Looking back on his past, on China's history and present situation, looking forward to the future, convinced him that the Party was after all a great and glorious Party, and must ultimately take the correct line.

Or was this merely hindsight? Since the day in '66 when he was "dragged out", he had been unable to believe what was happening. "Dragged out" — what a strangely evocative expression! A special political situation produced a special political jargon. These last few years had challenged the rules of the language. Would later generations understand the new terminology current today?

So he was awaiting a change, as eagerly as a racer awaits the start of a race. But life in the mountains had altered him, enabling him to exult in the first leeks picked that spring. He carefully cleaned them, inhaling their pungent fragrance. However, he couldn't make up his mind whether to ask Qiuwen over or not. He found this uncertainty exasperating.

What was that noise? Cattle, wind, the village children? No. A tractor maybe or a diesel engine? It was drawing nearer. Could it be a car that had lost its way? Those who travelled by car were respected, but that cut them off from the masses. Still, some people had to have cars. Rat-a-tat-tat — that sounded like chopping meat. He had no meat. Two eggs with the leeks would do fine: golden egg and vivid green leeks. Using eggs would take more oil, though, and their oil was strictly rationed. Rat-a-tat-tat — someone was knocking at the door.

A youngster. In army uniform, a red star on his cap.

He stood to attention, saluted. Zhang dropped the leeks. As he stood up he knocked the stool over.

Comrade Zhang Siyuan,
Please report to the Organization Department of the Provincial Committee before April 25.
Revolutionary greetings!

What does this mean? Comrade, do they acknowledge me as a comrade? The Organization Department. That's an important department, always staffed by the most reliable, most experienced cadres. And greetings — no wonder this soldier saluted me. The seal is that of the Political Affairs Office of the Revolutionary Committee. Why had he been sent for by this important body?

Anyway he had been sent for. His right to join in Party activities had not yet been restored. But he paid his Party fee every month. Since they hadn't expelled him, it was his right, not just his duty, to send the money in. And he'd sent the same amount as when he was drawing a high salary, though his present monthly allowance was only a third of that. This was provocative on his part. I'm still a high-ranking cadre, one third of my salary is just as much as you earn!

"Take a seat," he invited the soldier, his way of speaking, his smile and his bent back like those of a peasant. He was used to showing respect to the soldiers supporting the new leading bodies. Though they earned less than half than he did, their prestige was a hundred times greater.

The young soldier did not sit down. "There's a car outside, Comrade Zhang Siyuan," he said. "Can you

get your things ready to leave this afternoon? The
chairman said the sooner you go the better."

His respectful manner reminded Zhang of his
secretary and driver in the days when he was in power.

"Well. . . ." he drawled. A man's status affects the
tempo of his speech. It was nine years since he had
drawled like this, but it had been automatic. His face
flushed.

For nine years his heart had been like a placid lake.
Despite whirlpools and currents deep down, its surface
remained unruffled. There people could see their own
inverted reflections, often more impressive than in real
life.

Now the soldier's arrival ruffled the lake, set up
eddies. And so, willy-nilly, his consciousness changed
too.

He returned to his town. To the municipal committee
office, where he was appointed second in command.

"But my right to join in Party activities still hasn't
been restored," he pointed out.

"First take up your post," he was told.

His office had been redecorated, to cover up the scars
of the last years. The sight of the parquet floor and the
big hanging lamp brought tears to his eyes. Luckily no
one saw them. Paradise lost! he thought. For nine years
he had forgotten that floor, that lamp. For five years
his surroundings had been twisting mountain tracks,
shady trees, boulders and stone cottages with earthen
floors which had to be sprinkled with water. Too little
made the dust rise, too much made them muddy. At
night they lit kerosene lamps, the shades of which had
to be kept clean and bright. At first he had blown on
the shade before wiping it with a soft handkerchief, at

the risk of cutting his hand. Later he had learned to dip the handkerchief in alcohol. Then the cottage was bright as day. Besides, the blue sky was full of stars, many more than he saw in town. And they seemed to be much closer to the villagers on the mountain than to townsfolk. What he dreaded was the rain. In that storm, if not for Qiuwen, he might have died.

Here he did not have to dread the rain or night. At night in town his car kept out the rain. There was no winter in his centrally-heated office and flat. But without night there were no stars. Without rain there was no delight when a storm had passed. Without winter there was no immaculate snow. You couldn't have it both ways.

Many old comrades, friends, subordinates and former classmates called. He had suddenly become their hope, the focus of their attention, just as he had formerly been transformed into an untouchable.

"I've been longing to see you. I kept asking after you," said one, as if from his heart.

"I hesitated a long time. Now you're back in office, you must have so many callers. I didn't like to barge in. . . . Still we are old colleagues. Surely you won't forget us."

So it went on. His old colleagues in the municipal committee were jubilant at his rehabilitation. It augured well for their own reinstatement.

But there could be no return to the past which had been destroyed. Posters warned, "The capitalist-roaders are making a come-back" or "We refuse to take the old road." And behind all that seemed familiar he sensed a strange incompatibility. Drivers would not drive the buses, so that crowds of people waited in vain at the bus-stops. They said the drivers were playing poker, and the one who lost would have to take a bus out. Everywhere were posters, slogans, big criticism meetings, impassioned appeals. When a confectioner's set up a revolutionary leading group, that was declared a "great victory of Mao Zedong Thought". Under exultant red-character posters like this were piles of garbage and children begging for food. The street cleaners were on strike. And beggary increased along with empty boasts. More and more people were drinking, throwing parties. The terms used in drinking games had changed from the old ones, denounced by some Leftists as Confucian, into "Five for the five-starred flag, eight for the Eighth Route Army" and so forth. Life was a fantastic nightmare. What had made millions of people so gullible?

The municipal committee had also changed. Each time he went to his office his heart missed a beat. Had he come to the wrong place? Were they going to have him beaten? The signboard outside now was more ornate — the old one had been stolen to make a cupboard for somebody, as the town was short of wood — and the entrance was heavily guarded. It had to be. There were sentries too outside the gates of the Youth League and the Women's Federation.

Things had gone haywire. Cars had increased threefold but weren't enough to use, because leading cadres had increased fivefold. There were four section chiefs in the Organization Section, but they had only one secretary who did any work. Rumours were rife and superstition seemed rampant. There were feuding cliques. The Party had ceased to function normally, ruling out any possibility of criticism and self-criticism.

Public affairs were privately run, by pulling strings; and private affairs were attended to on the pretext of going out on public business. Blatant requests were made for Party membership, an official post, power. . . .

If this went on, our Party and our country were surely done for. The thought kept in him a fever of anxiety. Especially as his superior, the First Secretary who had rocketed up in the "cultural revolution", could do nothing but plot and do down other people.

On top of this, Meilan wanted them to re-marry. She wrote several letters which Zhang Siyuan ignored. When she telephoned for an appointment he said, "No need," then rang off, to cut short her protests. But one day, going home, he found her sitting there. She must have forced the door. Acting the part of a "rehabilitated" wife, she had stripped off his sheets to have them washed and put artifical flowers in the bedroom. Without a word Zhang Siyuan went back to his office, thankful now that the place was so heavily guarded. He took up a sheaf of documents. They called for "big criticism", going against the tide and all-round dictatorship, opposed emphasis on production, and claimed a great victory in the revolution in education. . . . His head whirled.

A return to yesterday was out of the question. He must spend his last years salvaging the future.

Qiuwen

He had fallen down in that storm. When he came to, he was lying in a ward of the commune hospital. Qiuwen, whose fame as a doctor had spread far and wide, was attending him herself. Not only had he damaged his spine, his soaking had resulted in pneumonia.

Soon after coming to this mountain village Zhang Siyuan had met Qiuwen, a graduate from the Shanghai Medical College. She was in her forties, tall, with big eyes and an oval face. She wore her glossy black hair in a bun like the old women in the village, but on her it looked attractive. Her clothes were always spotless, and she fairly raced along the mountain tracks. She was the last person you'd have expected to find in a village during the "cultural revolution", yet she was completely at home there. On easy terms with the villagers, she would take a puff or two at the pipes offered her. At weddings or funerals she would drink from cups already used.

He heard that she was divorced and living here with her daughter. It was hard for a woman on her own in the countryside, yet she had made friends with men and women alike, without giving rise to talk.

At first Zhang Siyuan was rather puzzled by her and didn't much like her, although he acknowledged her charm. There seemed something outré about the way she talked, walked, smoked and drank. But because she was a good doctor, on the best of terms with the villagers, he greeted her politely whenever they met. Later he discovered that Dongdong often called on her to borrow medical books. The boy needed some outside interests.

"You were delirious," Qiuwen had told him gently, not speaking in her usual bantering way. "As a high-ranking cadre, you probably had too much on your mind." Her mouth was covered by a surgical mask, but in her eyes were sympathy and understanding.

"In fact it's not a bad thing, people of your rank being sent to work with the peasants," she said on another occasion, ignoring the other patients in the ward. "Otherwise, no matter how often the papers appealed to cadres to come down to the countryside, you'd have stayed in your ivory tower. Right, Old Zhang?"

Zhang Siyuan felt like protesting. He had no ivory tower, not even a home now. But the appellation Old Zhang warmed his heart, just as when in his childhood his mother had called him Pebble. People need sympathy and understanding. So he took comfort each time the doctor told him, "Take this medicine and drink more water. You'll soon be better."

Dongdong brought him his meals every day: noodles, poached eggs, yam soup, millet congee. "Don't be so angry," he said. "I was only griping in my diary, but people who gripe do no harm. I was wrong that day. I shall always respect Li Dazhao and Fang Zhimin. Recently I've been thinking: Life isn't as fine as I thought when I was a kid, so it can't be as bad as it seems to me now either."

"So you've had a change of heart!" his father exclaimed.

"You can't call it that. I shall probably never understand you completely, just as you won't understand me. There'll always be a gap between people. That's why one of us will try to do down the other."

"Why bring me food every day then?"

"Aunt Qiuwen told me to. She said. . . ." Dongdong hesitated, as if uncertain whether to go on. "Aunt Qiuwen said: Your dad has had a hard time."

"You've discussed me with her?"

"Yes."

"Did you tell her about your mother?"

"Yes."

"What else?"

"I tell her everything. Why not? Is that disclosing state secrets?" Dongdong retorted.

"No, I think it's a good thing."

So Zhang Siyuan — Old Zhang rather — learned more about Qiuwen from Dongdong. Her husband had been made a Rightist in '57 and was still in a labour reform camp. It was for her daughter's sake, Dongdong thought, that she had divorced him. In fact she was waiting for his release. The work team sent here in '64 to uncover class enemies had initially had a bad impression of her and wanted to investigate her case. But all the commune members and village cadres were for her. She had gone of her own accord to tell the work team all about herself, keeping nothing back, and so had dispelled their suspicions.

Was all this protective colouring? Like a tree transplanted from elsewhere, she had acclimatized yet retained her unique characteristics. Her compliance, loquacity and optimism were a cover for her serious-mindedness and the cross she had to bear.

However, these things were not simply protective colouring. Genuinely well-disposed towards other people, she knew how to enjoy life. Concerned for the young and their love affairs, she was a new-style, tireless go-between. Were she just trying to cover up, how could her laughter be so genuine, so girlish?

But in good earnest she advised Zhang Siyuan, "You should learn all about our life here. When you go back to your post, don't forget the people in the mountains!"

When Zhang Siyuan brushed this aside as if he had no wish to reassume office, she chided, "Don't take that attitude. If I were you I'd be eager to go back. Are you getting paid all that money every month to hoe the fields here? You'll be rehabilitated and promoted."

"You're wrong." Zhang shook his head.

"Not a bit of it. What with deaths from natural and unnatural causes, there are fewer and fewer leading cadres left who have experience and real ability. That goes not only for you, but for university graduates too. If this revolution in education goes on for ten more years, there'll be so many illiterates in China, anyone with primary schooling will be a sage! And cadres like yourself will be virtually impossible to find. You can't leave the running of the country to the peasants! But if you don't run things well, the folk here, and outside too, are going to curse you!"

Zhang got the message then. Governing the country was their inescapable duty. A change was bound to come. The present situation would be reversed. He had not suspected Qiuwen of such political acumen. But shall I live to see it? We always say nobody's indispensable, and I've been out of things all these years.

Qiuwen's prediction came true before long. In '75, while cleaning leeks, Zhang Siyuan was recalled to the city. In '77, after the toppling of the "gang of four", he was promoted to be vice-secretary of the Provincial Committee. In '79, he was transferred to Beijing, with the post of vice-minister in the State Council.

On the Road

At last he had left the élitist Ministers' Mansion, a high-rise building for cadres of his rank. A fleet of limousines was usually parked in front of it. Ordinary people were kept away by the sentries. It wasn't easy leaving his flat now that he had grown used to it. Although he had long planned to revisit the mountain village, there seemed something holding him back. The thought of leaving his familiar routine made him uneasy and rather exasperated, like someone accustomed to three meals a day who is suddenly made to switch to two or four, or like a fish which has suddenly decided to go ashore. Tonight he was sleeping here. Where would he be sleeping tomorrow or the day after? The evening before his departure his mind was troubled. Invisible hands seemed to be holding him back. A voice urged: Drop it. Aren't you sitting pretty here? You're nearly sixty, with an important post. You've no right to get carried away by emotion. Why look for trouble?

But finally he left the Ministers' Mansion. More than that, he refused to travel by plane or soft sleeper, refused to let his secretary notify the local authorities of his arrival. His secretary hinted that this was childish and inconsiderate. He all but asked: Have you taken leave of your senses?

Now the train was pulling out to the accompaniment of a broadcast song. He had left his secretary, driver and black limousine. The whistle let out a piercing blast — they were off. The carriage attendant asked urgently, "Whose is this luggage?" As Zhang Siyuan closed his eyes an irate mother slapped her naughty child and it started howling. When he opened his eyes the carriage was flooded with sunshine. The wind ruffled his greying hair. Someone had opened the window. He relaxed, feeling free — a butterfly again.

"Your ticket!" the attendant ordered, reaching for it.

Under the blue railway worker's cap, her young face showed impatience. She wouldn't have spoken like this to a first-class passenger. Zhang produced his ticket. The railway uniforms and the PLA uniforms should be improved; people had been dressing better the last two years, but these uniforms were unchanged. They ought to be made more attractive. . . .

A fat fellow with a red nose, bare-chested, plumped himself down beside him, making the wooden sleeper creak. "Like a game of poker?" He had a Shandong accent and his breath reeked of onions. In the first class. . . .

The first class would be much better than this, of course. But he liked this carriage. Liked the grim-faced attendant. Here she was again hard at work mopping the floor. He liked the PLA soldiers on the two berths above him. As soon as the train started they had gone to sleep — how soundly young people sleep! He liked the cadre opposite, who was smoking a cheap cigarette and thrust one on him. Why were tobacco and drink considered so bad? This comrade had no intention of asking a favour. Then there was the mother whose child was running up and down, putting on an act for perfect strangers. Children made life more worth living. Dongdong talked of the gap between people, but they could still love each other.

Yes, over four years had passed since he resumed office in '75. The first year had been hard and disillusioning; the second, a year of bitter grief and wild excitement. They had been two troubled years of endless problems, but progress had been made. Looking back he was amazed by the speed and scope of the changes, impatient with those bureaucrats stuck in a rut. He had been too busy to meet ordinary people like those in this carriage. Even if he went down to the grass-roots level, his status set him apart. But he couldn't return with a whole retinue to the mountain village, presenting himself like a high official to Dongdong and Qiuwen. Although he knew it wasn't wrong for him or his colleagues to ride in cars, live in the Ministers' Mansion or travel soft, he could not, dared not go back as if he were superior to ordinary people.

Actually, even travelling by a hard sleeper didn't satisfy the egalitarians. The majority of people travelled on hard seats. This journey would take over seventy hours and they would sit it out for seventy hours. The Chinese people are second to none in their patience, fortitude and industry. Then why can so few of them afford even to travel hard thirty years after Liberation? Doesn't that make you blush? You must work harder. Look at the ordinary passengers at each station as, with crates and packs on their backs, they help along old folk and children.

They are Old Zhang, Old Li, Old Wang and Old Liu. Well, for two weeks he could be Old Zhang again. After his rehabilitation he had often recalled his life as Old Zhang. Sometimes he wondered: Why can't there be another Zhang Siyuan called Old Zhang, able to live in that remote, lovely, rain-swept mountain village with all its trees, grass, birds and bees? When he stooped to get into his limousine, was Old Zhang gathering firewood on the mountain amid bird song? When, drawling, he addressed meetings, was Old Zhang joking with the village women during a break in the fields? He didn't drawl to impress people, far from it; but when he expressed his views on extremely complex problems they had to be clear and correct. He had to think what he was saying, and give his listeners time to understand and digest Vice-minister Zhang's instructions. So this drawl of his was necessary and natural. The other Zhang Siyuan — Old Zhang — never drawled. He spoke rapidly, fluently, being younger and stronger than Vice-minister Zhang. When Vice-minister Zhang entertained foreign guests, helping them to delicacies and the best drinks, his other self was eating a bowl of congee, beans and pickles on a rickety stool in a smoky little cottage. Brother Shuanfu liked to boast that his were "vintage" pickles which he had salted in '29, boiling them every summer and adding vegetables and brine every autumn. When Vice-minister Zhang handled problems relating to personnel (which nowadays occupied so much of his time), choosing his words with care and doing his best to stick to principles, show consideration and forestall criticism, Old Zhang was listening raptly while Brother Shuanfu related the history of his pickles.

Now he had left Vice-minister Zhang in Beijing. Let him attend those interminable meetings, read those endless documents. After ten years of chaos he was working hard for the Party and the people, for the mountain village, Old Zhang and Brother Shuanfu. Whatever the faults of the present policy, he couldn't think of a better way to serve the people. Vice-minister Zhang could tell Old Zhang this with a clear conscience.

He accepted a strong cigarette from the man sitting opposite, not liking to produce his filter-tipped brand. Not that this would have caused surprise, because nowadays even factory apprentices took two packets of good cigarettes with them when they travelled, to give them "face". His present social status was determined by the hard sleeper on which he was sitting. He accepted the invitation to play poker, a game, like chess, which he had learned only after being labelled a counter-revolutionary. Like other bored passengers, he pored over the timetable, as if he was going to be transferred to be a train dispatcher. He intercepted the little boy who was running up and down, gave him a sweet and played with him. He had meant to do some reading on the train, but each time he took out his book he was interrupted. Never mind. Old Zhang was on a par with other people and had no extra duties, so what was the hurry? Brother Shuanfu reasoned: Everyone has to die, so what's the hurry? Take things easy, and you can delay your death. Very true. But although Old Zhang was relaxed and a free agent, he might make no mark in history. Every gain involved a loss, and the loss was too costly.

There were other minor yet tiresome drawbacks. Old Zhang had to stand in a queue to get into the station or on to the train, to go to the restaurant car, the lavatory or the washroom. Old Zhang was used to queueing but Vice-minister Zhang resented it. And he had to put up with rudeness. A chubby little boy kept rushing through the carriage. Old Zhang barred his way and offered him a sweet, but the child knocked it on to the floor cursing, "Damn you!" This set all the passengers laughing. Zhang Siyuan, the vice-minister uppermost, flushed in annoyance. When struggled against and cursed, he had had to accept it, but as a vice-minister he couldn't take this.

"Don't swear!" he snapped.

"Why not?" the boy retorted. "I'll tell my dad not to give you anything to eat."

As his father was a cook on the train, the passengers roared with laughter, commenting, "Good for you, kid! You understand the meaning of 'power'."

But worse was yet to come. After leaving the train he had to travel two days by long-distance coach. The driver treated his passengers like dirt. He was insolent and domineering.

The first time they stopped for the night, he put up in a big room for forty-two people, reeking of smoke and sweat. Six forty-watt fluorescent lights stayed on all night. At midnight the innkeeper woke everyone up to check if they had paid or not. He spent a sleepless night. It was too impractical, travelling like this. He should have listened to his secretary. If the Provincial Committee had sent a car to meet him, this two days' journey would have taken less than a day. After all, he was getting on now, he wasn't Old Zhang any more....

The next day, however, his morale improved. He boarded the bus exulting that he was still as tough as the labouring masses. At the same time he was aware of a sense of superiority. He seemed to hear someone comment: Vice-minister Zhang is just slumming for a few days. . . . He frowned.

Still, one incident proved too much to take. At noon that day when he joined a long queue to buy lunch, a tall hooligan jumped the queue just ahead of him, sizing him up as old and weak. This was a personal affront.

"Why don't you queue, comrade?" he asked.

No response.

"Go and queue up!" Zhang bellowed, tugging at his sleeve.

The tall fellow glanced at him contemptuously. "Don't talk rubbish!" He raised his fist. "Who says I've not queued up?"

"Did he queue or not?" Zhang asked the bystanders, expecting them to back him. But to his amazement and anger, nobody said a word. Some averted their eyes.

"You're the one who didn't queue!" The hooligan shoved Zhang away, spoiling for a fight. But how could Zhang fight him? How he wished his secretary, bodyguard or driver were here! Had his bodyguard been there to draw his pistol, or his secretary telephoned the police, this hooligan might well have dropped on his knees. Then the onlookers would have applauded. . . . But now this was out of the question. If he put up a fight he would be licked. Would this have enraged me so when I was in disgrace? This question had a sobering effect.

The trials of travelling! The common people had troubles of their own, no less than a "top cadre". It shouldn't have been a case of Zhuangzi dreaming he was a butterfly or a butterfly dreaming it was Zhuangzi, but of an ox dreaming it was a tractor or a tractor dreaming it was an ox. How many people could flit idly through life? When he was six his dad had fled from home with him to escape bandits, and they had spent a night in the stable of a hostel for carters. At sixty he still remembered the sound of the horses champing in the stillness of the night, a bitterly cold night. This was his most vivid memory of his childhood. In the war against Japan they had often slept in the maize fields, where on summer nights they heard the creak of maize as it shot up, drawing strength from the soil, rain and air. On the Long March he had even dozed off while marching. At the command to halt, soldiers often bumped their heads on the man in front.

It was easy to complain. That was the fashion. Some Chinese at the end of the seventies seemed to feel they couldn't get through the day without griping. Well, he had plenty to gripe about on this trip. Too bad he wasn't a writer, or he'd have had ample material for an essay just from the eating-house. By adding a few characters and some sarcastic comments, he could have written a short story of exposure. He might win fame and join the Writers' Association, able to throw his weight about as a hero more astute than other people. It was much easier and pleasanter to write denouncing an eating-house than to run an eating-house well. But what problems would that solve? We can't spend all our lives griping. The gripes of a man with no sense of social responsiblity are worthless. He had advised the cadres in his ministry: Let's divide up our eight-hour working day into four hours for griping, four for work. And when we work, let's make a good job of it. The result may be more efficient than eight hours spent slacking. Of course he had said this in anger.

He thought of his responsibilities, the responsibilities of everyone. Despite crudity and poverty, the trains and buses were running, taking countless passengers to their destination.

A Shower of Dates

Here he was at last! The pleasure of arrival makes up for the hardship of travel. Just as success compensates us for hard struggles. One more hill to climb, then two huge boulders to bypass, and there was the village bus-stop. In the four years and more of his absence these boulders had not changed. They looked indestructible as they welcomed him back, just as if he had never been away, had never become a vice-minister. As the bus drew up, the first sight to meet his eyes was Dongdong and the high-tension wires above his head. Dongdong looked taller, sturdier. Now a primary school teacher in the county town, he had come back to meet his father.

"So you have electricity?" Zhang asked.

"Yes, electric lights and electric power," Dongdong told him.

Father and son strolled to the old apricot tree, beneath which Old Zhang had often smoked his pipe. Now he gave his son a filter-tipped cigarette, which Dongdong accepted with a curl of his lips. By the apricot tree was a spring. To keep it clean, two flagstones covered it. Haiyun had loved to sing that Polish song *Only Bad Girls Dirty a Spring*. They basked in the early winter sun, out of the wind. Look, green grass is sprouting between the withered leaves beside the spring. Do they realize winter is coming? He raised the flag-stones to take a drink. The water was still clear and sweet. Looking up, he saw a tailor, a man he had had few dealings with before. His old-fashioned spectacles made him appear as ancient as the two boulders. But the tailor recognized him at a glance.

"Isn't it Secretary Zhang? What brings you back to our gully? Here, let me take your bag. . . . Fine, we're all fine, thanks to Chairman Hua and the brilliant leadership of the Party. Are you on a tour of inspection or will you stay awhile? That'll buck everyone up; it shows your concern. . . ,"

What a contrast between past and present! This obsequious way of talking set Zhang's teeth on edge.

Luckily this was the only villager whose attitude to him had changed. Brother Shuanfu was not like that. "Zhang!" he yelled from a distance, using only his surname, as was his custom. His wife when she saw Zhang shed tears.

"I never thought you'd come back. Never thought I'd live to see this day! Things are much better with us now. We have three pigs, five goats and fifteen hens. Twenty-five to start with, but two of them were cocks, kept pecking each other till their combs were bloodied, and I had to kill the one who came off worst. Then nine hens died. Dr Qiuwen gave them injections. She can treat hens as well as pigs — though the commune does have a vet. The state pays more for our grain too, as well as for walnuts, almonds, dates and honey. We have electric lights and a loudspeaker. But the men in the grain depot keep downgrading our grain — it hurts them to part with more money. And we often have power cuts, so we've hung on to our kerosene lamps, but kerosene's in short supply. Last year we made over four hundred yuan. Bought a pretty set of china. Have you been promoted? Kept well? Been to Beijing? Seen the heads of the Central Committee? Why don't cadres come down any more? Some used to come every winter. Even though they put us through the mill we miss them. Do send some to tell us what's going on in the world."

The fifteen hens were promptly reduced to thirteen. The scraggy old peasant woman, nearing seventy, deftly grabbed two and carried them inside. Feathers flew in all directions. Then the chicken, chopped up, sizzled in the pan. Rolls of white flour were steamed. Next appeared leek shoots dried in the autumn, beans, dried eggplant, salted pork. Meanwhile many villagers had dropped in. Five of them insisted that Zhang should have a meal with them later. He missed his secretary who made his appointments and left it to Dongdong to fix different times for each.

He felt in his element, as if he had never left. The local accent, the villagers' warmth were unchanged. He could walk into any household, pick up their chopsticks and eat, sleep on anyone's *kang*. Even the old dogs had not forgotten him, but ran over wagging their tails. He had brought the villagers sweets, ball-point pens and pictures, but had forgotten to bring the dogs a bone. Only one pup didn't know him and barked till its master swore, "What's come over you, barking at our Old Zhang? Shut up!" The pup slunk away, its tail between its legs, although it had only been trying to do its duty.

Though many people asked what his job was now, and exclaimed in pleased amazement at his promotion, no one treated him as a "superior". Speaking to them, he didn't drawl or gesticulate, pace up and down with his hands behind his back or weigh his every word. How good it felt not being an official! You can't have friendship without equality, can't grow crops without soil.

There were red dates here, as sweet as those of his childhood. His family had had a date tree before he was Zhang Siyuan, Instructor Zhang or Secretary Zhang, when his mother called him Pebble. Beating down dates was one of the treats of childhood. From the boughs beaten with bamboo poles the dates came raining down. His small friends gathered round to eat them, whooping as they filled their baskets and carried them off. Some dates rolled into the ditches or into the grass, and those were always the sweetest and plumpest, free from maggots. The discovery of one of these crafty dates made him and his playmates cheer. What a boisterous childhood! Grubby cheeks streaked with sweat, running noses, smiling faces.... Perhaps the desire for equality and friendship, for a better life for all, had been in the hearts of those children picking dates. And did the strength and the dynamic teachings of the great Marxists stem from the hearts of boisterous little children?

Now, grey-haired Vice-minister Zhang Siyuan was back in the boisterous atmosphere of his childhood. The first day, wherever he went, he was surrounded by villagers old and young, bombarded with questions, laughter, good wishes complaints ... like a shower of sweet, ripe red dates.

He had no time that day for a good talk with Dongdong or Qiuwen. When his eyes met Qiuwen's in the crowd, he was as excited as a child. He had never known anyone like her. She had won through so much grief; she was like a big sister pleased to see the little ones happily picking up dates, like the solitary moon lighting up the leafless date tree. He shivered.

That night he slept with his son and an old peasant, replete with good food, drinks, and the warmth of his welcome. In a dream he relived the fifty-nine years of his life. As a shepherd boy he had fought the landlord's brat. The Red Army had come, singing. In a hail of bullets he had thrown his first hand-grenade. . . . Under a red flag he had joined the Party. He had gladly risked his life, sure that the revolution would rain down happiness like dates on every household.

Summer. A white, short-sleeved blouse, a blue skirt. Her school's telephone number was 4583. Taking the call she was nervous, knowing without being told who was phoning her. Her white figure flashed past. Had she too gone to the mountains? To which commune, which village? That talk of her death had been false. You are still alive, don't leave me, I've something to tell you. Weren't you notified that your name had been cleared? 4583 — why does no one answer the phone? He slammed down the receiver. Sobbed. Imprisonment, release, driving in a limousine through Beijing. Travelling first-class from Beijing to Wuhan. Flying in a jet plane through the blue sky and white clouds. The sky above bluer than sapphire, the clouds below whiter than snow. A shower of dates. Pamphlets. Fists. My heart — quick, give me some medicine, an injection! The draft report will be sent round tomorrow for comments.

This would never do, at his age, letting his fancies run away with him. But weren't they the torch which had lighted his way forward? He had hesitated about coming here, had been reluctant to leave the Minister's Mansion. But here is the real Zhang Siyuan. He hasn't changed. He belongs to the mountains. What? Time already? I'll go right away. Endless meetings, even in dreams. Comrades, the situation is excellent. We need stability and unity, need to introduce reforms and cut down on redundancy; we can't go on having more officers than soldiers.

The Gap

The weather too welcomed Zhang Siyuan's return by remaining fine for days. Dongdong accompanied him through the terraced fields, orchards and vegetable pots. Everything there was unchanged. They tramped through prickly wild dates, avoiding the hunters' traps, till they came to the nursery. The pine seedlings they had planted five years before in the rain were now knee-high. They would grow up to shade several generations to come. The thought warmed his heart.

But he and Dongdong did not see eye to eye. Dongdong showed unusual consideration for him, advising him to exercise and rest more, to go to the seaside each summer. Yes, Dongdong had grown up. Why not go to Beijing, his father asked. You've every reason. I'm getting old now, we ought to be together. To his surprise, Dongdong flatly refused.

Why not?

I don't want to be the son of a high-ranking cadre.

What do you mean? Can't high-ranking cadres have children? We've devoted our whole lives to the revolution, for the people's sake.

Zhang was worked up, but Dongdong kept calm.

I admire your generation, but you should face up to facts. There's a lot of hostility to the children of high-ranking cadres. Now wait a bit. We want to put our lives to some purpose too, like your generation, to be pioneers. But all you want of us, all you allow us, is to follow in your steps, to be your successors and take over from you. Well, that's impossible. All these years I've been educated by my parents, teachers, the Youth League, the peasants, and the higher-ups. Now the time's come for us to educate ourselves, to make our way in life.

That's one-sided, empty talk. China's suffered too much from such talk. It's the Party's policy, not high-falutin talk, that has made life better for the peasants. We're not living in a vacuum. You can't start again from scratch. You don't understand the situation or history. Your half-baked ideas, if acted on, would only hold things up or result in bloodshed. History is an unbroken chain, and taking over from old revolution-aries doesn't mean following a beaten track. We're trying to blaze a new trail. What China needs is not wild talk but honest-to-goodness work. We must all of us go on learning as long as we live....

Dongdong spotted a hawthorn tree with five bright berries still unpicked, and threw stones to bring them down. He showed no interest in his father's line of reasoning.

"I'm going back to the county town tomorrow," he announced. "We can have another talk there. Please don't take offence. One reason I'm not keen to live with you is because I don't like the way you lecture me. Mother wasn't like that. Nine tenths of the time she just looked after me. But then she was a weak character, you're a strong one. I'd rather bash out my brains than knuckle under to you. Maybe I'll visit you next sum-mer.... Won't that do?"

Zhang Siyuan fell silent, looking at the pine saplings on the opposite hill as he ate the two hawberries given him by his son. The late afternoon sun made the sap-lings cast long shadows.

The Parting

Back in '77, Zhang had learned of the death of Qiuwen's husband in the labour camp. He had written her a letter of condolence, told her of his own difficulties, his resolve to soldier on.

He had received no answer. That was the third time he had written to Qiuwen. The first had been a note enclosed in his letter to Dongdong just after his reinstatement. "I often remember my days in the village," he had said. "I am most grateful for the medical care and other help you gave me, and for your kindness to Dongdong. Best wishes to you and your daughter." This had also gone unanswered, but Dongdong had written, "Aunt Qiuwen sends her best regards."

The second letter was written in the spring of '76, when he had to go along with the campaign against Deng Xiaoping. In that political climate he wrote fearfully, using the language of editorials. "We must trust that Chairman Mao's revolutionary line will win the final victory."

"The peasants welcome you back here any time to remould yourself through labour," she had replied. "Materialists are fearless. Communism is a militant philosophy."

Zhang Siyuan had understood. The recollection of Qiuwen, Dongdong and the villagers had a steadying effect on him.

In '77 he felt tempted to go and see Qiuwen again, to ask her to marry him. She was a strange character, combining the sturdiness of a pine with the pliancy of a willow. In the village she had shown herself the stronger of the two. Besides, since his refusal to take

Meilan back, many of his old comrades-in-arms and above all their wives, concerned about his welfare, kept thrusting photographs at him, eager to act as go-betweens. Finally, in exasperation, he announced that he had found someone in the village where he had worked. He would go to fetch her, and could dispense with their good offices. Thereupon his friends stopped thrusting photographs at him. Instead, they kept asking him the date of his wedding.

"Maybe, judging by Chinese conventions, I shouldn't propose to you. Maybe you'll be angry. But I've wanted for years to ask you. When I had pneumonia and was not so old, you gave me strength and courage. . . . But for your sake I hid my feelings."

"Thank you," said Qiuwen bluntly, as if amused.

"I've never met another woman like you. High-minded but easy-going, sharp-tongued but warm--hearted. . . ."

"Are you trying to make me out a paragon?"

"This isn't a laughing matter," he protested. "And I feel you understand me, even like me."

Qiuwen avoided his eyes.

"I'm in real difficulties, yoked like an ox. When problems crop up, I often think if I had you to advise me and back me up . . . my work would be much easier."

". . . ."

"I came this time because of you. You must have guessed that. Come back with me. You can choose any job you like. And your daughter will live with us, that goes without saying. . . ."

"Us?" snapped Qiuwen. "Why should I be your

adviser? Why should I leave my work, my post, my life here with the peasants to be a minister's wife?"

". . . ."

"See, you think only of yourself. High officials always consider themselves more important than other people, right? Not for a second has it occurred to you to leave Beijing, leave your official post, and come here to be my adviser, support and friend.   Can you deny it?"

"Well, we can consider that alternative."

"Consider that alternative? Official jargon! Sorry. Didn't my reaction just now prove that I'm not as good as you imagined? Your job is a hundred times more important than mine. You can't back out of it. I support you and your colleagues. You're the cream, the hope of our country. I believe you can make up for all the time you lost. I wish you success. But I can't go with you. I'm too used to running wild. The life of a minister's wife would stifle me. I'd be quite out of place."

"Then do you intend to stay here all your life? Are you not out of your element here?"

"No, I feel at home here. That's why I admire you. You can be a vice-minister yet come back to the mountains to muck in with us. But what you're asking of me is fantastic. I'm not so adaptable, I'm just a village doctor. Don't forget us! If you keep us in your heart, everything will be fine. Thanks, though." She sounded rather shocked. "Just do more good for the people and don't harm them.   Then the people won't forget you."

His own throat constricted, he walked slowly away. Qiuwen didn't see him off. He regretted now not having taken a longer look at her solid chair, her white deal table, her lamp, her books, her washstand, straw hat and stethoscope. These things were lucky to be with her all the time.

The villagers went on entertaining him. With his stomach and head he conducted a social investigation. Beancurd and vermicelli, cider and vinegar — they made these themselves. Fresh and salted eggs, preserved and salted duck eggs, brought them in an extra income. Fried cakes of flour with honey were their favourite sweet.... What other problems have you? What other opinions? ... We're afraid things may change. If the policy doesn't change and we don't mess things up, our life will get steadily better. We're counting on you! We peasants have faith in you.

After eating and drinking their fill they encouraged each other.

Then he had to say goodbye. Vice-minister Zhang's secretary was very able. A week after Zhang Siyuan had travelled incognito to the mountain village to share in the life of the people, his secretary rang up the local authorities. In no time, leading cadres and an escort arrived there by car. Zhang looked carefully around. It dawned on him that the villagers understood him better than his son. The warmth of their reception hadn't been because they didn't know of his promotion or that he was fully entitled to a car and escort. They knew all this, but they also knew the sort of man he was. Their attitude to him hadn't changed because they still trusted him. His eyes filled with tears. This gave an added value to all the experiences of the past week.

People thronged round to see him off. "Don't forget us!" That was all they asked. How could he ever forget or disappoint them? Tears in his eyes, he took his seat by the driver, there considered as the seat of honour,

He left his heart in the village, yet had the village in his heart as he drove away. Had his visit been in vain? Far from it. He had found his true self. In the county town he said goodbye to Dongdong, then drove to the provincial capital. No queueing this time, of course. No wild urchins or hooligans, no reek of onions, no staying in a rowdy doss-house. How well I'm being looked after. Isn't it my duty to see to it that everybody has a better life?

After a night in the best provincial hotel he took a plane, travelling first-class. "No smoking" and "Fasten your seat belts" flashed on. Then the engine roared and they were airborne. The mountain village was left far behind; ahead, many tricky problems awaited him. But he was not afraid. A uniformed air hostess brought him jasmine tea, chocolate, chewing-gum, picture postcards. . . . The plane banked to change course as they reached the right altitude, higher by far than a butterfly could fly. The steady roar of the engine was reassuring. As the cabin warmed up he adjusted a switch above his head, and cold air blew on his face. He stared down through the porthole at China outspread below. He loved the sunlight and shadows of each range of hills, the chequered fields, the roads criss-crossing like a spider's web. If only this dear country, mountain villages and all, could speed ahead like a plane! How long will folk go on pickling vegetables as they did in '29? Below was a cloud-bank, a sea of white and grey. No matter how high the plane flew, it came from the earth and must return to the earth. Men and butterflies alike were the earth's children. He switched off the air conditioning, lowered the back of his seat and fell sound asleep.

The Bridge

He ate a bowl of chicken noodles, a steamed roll, some ham. He stretched, lit a cigarette, puffed at it, then stubbed it out. No poet, he had no time to let his fancy wander. He had to work away like an ox or tractor. To do a good job of work was everything. Having changed into his pyjamas, he went into the bathroom for a shave. His face under the light was shining. Running a bath, he tried humming that Hong Kong tune he had heard on the road, then burst out laughing and switched to a folk song. A good bath always refreshed him. He believed he could carry on working hard till each family in the country had a white, gleaming bathtub. He dried himself with a towel, his skin pink in the lamplight. He wasn't old yet. Warm red blood coursed in his veins.

Switching off the lights he went to the sitting-room to smoke a cigarette and turned on the radio. Feeling as buoyant as a butterfly, he walked with a light step to the balcony and opened the French window. The cool night air seemed like the breeze in the mountain. His coat draped over his shoulders, he stepped out. The stars in the sky and the city lights intermingled. He gazed at the silent, distant stars, the same as the stars in the mountains.

There was manifestly a link, a bridge between past, present and future; between father, son and grandson; between mountain boulders and this Ministers' Mansion between Qiuwen's glance, Dongdong's cussedness, the waist drums of '49 and the demonstrations of '76; between Pebble, Instructor Zhang, Secretary Zhang, Old Zhang and Vice-minister Zhang. This bridge existed, linking life and death. He himself bore witness to that. This bridge must be kept in good repair, unobstructed. He longed to see Haiyun, Qiuwen, Dongdong and Shuanfu's family again. He was looking forward eagerly to the future.

He did some exercises and breathed deeply. Was that the telephone? Stepping back into the warm, bright sitting-room he drew the light green curtain, then went into his study to answer the phone. It was the minister, asking about his trip.

"Mission accomplished?"

"Pretty well," he answered cheerfully.

Then the minister briefed him about an important meeting to be held in two days. He was asked to prepare a report.

He rang off and went to his desk. His secretary had already brought the most urgent documents and letters here. There was a list of problems requiring immediate attention. He picked up a pencil to go through this material, immersing himself in it. It seemed many people were watching him, supporting him, hoping great things of him.

Tomorrow the pressure of work would be even greater.

Translated by Gladys Yang

The Eyes of Night

ALL the street lamps were switched on, of course, at the same time. However Chen Gao felt as if there were two streams of light shooting out in opposite directions above his head. There seemed to be no end to them. Locust trees cast their simple, yet stalwart shadows on to the pavements, as did people waiting at the bus stop, each having more than one shadow.

Everywhere, there were heavy vehicles, cars, trolleybuses, bicycles, and the hooting, voices and laughter typical of a big city at night — full of life. He saw occasional neon lights and barber's poles. Also permed hair, long hair, high-heeled shoes and frocks. In the air hung the fragrance of toilet water and face cream. Though the city women had just begun to pay a little attention to their appearance, they had already outraged certain people. This was interesting.

Chen Gao had left this city more than twenty years before, to live in a remote small town, where one-third of the street lamps were never lit and the rest had no electricity for part of the month. Nobody knew whether this was through neglect or lack of coal. However, it did not matter much, because people began their work at dawn and finished at dusk, like peasants following the customs of their ancestors. After six o'clock when all the offices, factories, shops and halls were closed, people stayed at home, looking after their children, smoking, washing or chatting.

Along came a blue bus. The conductress was speaking into a microphone, while the passengers jostled to get off. Chen Gao and some others squeezed their way on to the bus. It was packed. However, Chen felt pleased. The conductress, a rosy-cheeked girl, had a clear, resonant voice. She could have been the announcer for the song and dance ensemble in his remote town. After she had switched on a small light, she began selling tickets. Then she switched the light off. Outside the window, street lamps, trees, buildings and people flashed past. The bus approached another stop. Once again, as the conductress announced the name of the next stop, the light was switched on and passengers began to elbow their way to the doors.

Two young men in workers' overalls got on, continuing their heated discussion. One of them said, "The key question is democracy, democracy. . . ." Though he had only been a week in this city, Chen realized that democracy was a very popular topic, just like legs of mutton to the people where he lived. Here, perhaps, there was a good supply of meat, so people did not have to worry about trifles like joints of mutton. This was wonderful Chen thought, smiling.

But there was no contradiction between democracy and legs of mutton. Without democracy, the mutton on your plate would be snatched away. A democracy which could not bring more succulent legs of mutton to his townsfolk was empty talk. Chen was in the city attending a writers' conference on short stories and plays. After the fall of the "gang of four", he had published five or six short stories. Some critics said that he had become more mature, more versatile. But most people held that these works were not up to his earlier standard. One who paid too much attention to legs of mutton could not produce good stories. Knowing the importance of and need for mutton, however, was progress. On his way to the conference, he had been delayed for over an hour by a train accident in a small railway station. In a hurry to sell his mutton, a black-marketeer had risked crossing the railway tracks underneath a stationary train. Unfortunately, the brakes failed and the train had moved, killing the poor fellow. This was still preying on Chen's mind.

In the past, he had always been the youngest at such conferences, but now he was among the middle-aged, looking a provincial, with a dark, weather-beaten face. The young participants expressed fresh, bold, shrewd and lively ideas in their speeches, which were thought-provoking, stimulating and inspiring. No one seemed very interested in literary and art problems, though the chairman did his best to make them keep to the main subject. What they discussed most were the conditions responsible for the emergence of the "gang of four", feudalism, democracy, the law, morality and so on. More and more youngsters, for example, were dancing to the music of electric guitars and fooling about in parks. They talked about what the parks' administrators were doing to control them. Chen also gave his view which, comparatively speaking, was low-keyed. "We must begin gradually," he said, "starting from ourselves." It would be a wonder if half or one-fifth or even one-tenth of the good suggestions raised at the conference were realized. Chen was excited yet perplexed.

The bus reached the terminal, but it was still quite full. Everyone seemed rather relaxed and paid little attention to the conductress, who was asking to see their tickets with a note of irritation in her voice. Chen, like all those from the provinces, held high his ticket, but the girl did not even glance at him. Then he politely held it out to her, but she did not take it.

Having got off the bus, he took out his address book and leafed through it for the one he wanted. When he asked a passerby where the place was, several others volunteered the information. So in this respect, at least, city people still showed their traditional courtesy. Having thanked them, he left the brightly-lit terminal. After turning a few corners, he found himself lost in the labyrinth of a new housing estate.

It was not that the layout of the buildings was complicated. It was too simple! All the six-storeyed blocks looked identical. Each balcony was crammed with all sorts of things. From each window shone a yellow lamp or a white fluorescent light. Even the sounds coming from them were similar. A football match between China and some other country was being shown on television, and probably the Chinese team had just scored a goal. The boisterous cheers of the spectators and the football fans sitting before their TV sets mingled with the familiar voice of Zhang Zhi, the sports commentator. From other windows came the sounds of hammering, chopping, children yelling, or adults scolding.

All these noises, lights and the profusion of things packed into those blocks as identical as matchboxes struck Chen as rather strange and unfamiliar, even rather ridiculous. And the trees, as tall as the buildings, added a touch of mystery. In his little town, one heard mostly dogs barking at night. Chen knew them all and their masters. And lorries rumbled along the street, their headlights blinding people.

Chen regretted getting into this maze. "I shouldn't have turned off that brightly-lit street," he thought. "I shouldn't have left that crowded, cheerful bus. How wonderful it was riding with so many people along a wide boulevard!" But now he was all alone in the dark. He should have stayed in the hostel, where he could have gone on discussing with some youngsters how to solve the problems resulting from the years of misrule of the "gang of four" or talked about other countries, over plates of lobster crisps, boiled peanuts and some cool, refreshing beer. Instead, he had travelled all the way by bus to this outlandish place to ask a favour of a perfect stranger. There was nothing strange about the favour itself, which was routine, necessary. The problem was that Chen was not the right person for the job. He would rather go up the stage and dance the role of the prince in *Swan Lake*, despite his limp, which, hardly noticeable, was a reminder of the "cultural revolution".

His depression brought back sad memories of the day he had left this city over twenty years ago. He had parted company with his friends for publishing several short stories which were condemned as "going too far". In fact now they were considered not sharp enough.

According to what people had just told him, the building ahead, not too far away, was the one he was looking for. Unfortunately there was a ditch for laying sewage pipes barring his way, too wide to jump across. He searched for a plank to cross it, but to his annoyance found none. To skirt round it or jump over? "I'm not that old," he said to himself. He backed a few paces and then ran forward. Confound it! Just as he took off, one of his feet stuck in the sand and he tumbled into the ditch. Fortunately, there was nothing hard or sharp at the bottom. Still, it took him more than ten minutes to recover from the shock and pain. Smiling, he dusted himself down and climbed out — into a puddle! He hurriedly withdrew his foot. But too late! His shoe and sock were soaked through. He felt as uncomfortable as when you eat rice with grit in it. Looking up, he saw a lonely orange-coloured lamp hung on a slanting pole, like a big exclamation mark on a big blackboard.

As he approached the building he again heard cheers and whistles from its windows. Perhaps the foreign team had scored. Reaching an entrance, he looked closely at the number and decided that this was the place. However, he still hesitated. He waited, hoping someone would pass by to confirm it.

Before he had set off for this city, the head of his organization had given him a letter of introduction and asked him to look up a certain company manager. "We were pals in the army," he told Chen. "The letter explains everything. Something's wrong with our Shanghai car. The driver and some comrades in our administration office have tried everywhere to get it repaired, but no one can fix it because they've no spare parts. Now this friend of mine is in charge of motor maintenance and he once assured me that if I needed our car repaired, I should go to him. So you go and find him. Send me a telegram when it's settled."

There was nothing unusual in asking a friend, a

comrade-in-arms, to do a favour. Why shouldn't someone in authority ask someone else with power and influence to repair his unit's car, which was, after all, state property? There was no reason to refuse, and Chen, who knew the importance of legs of mutton, never doubted the necessity of the errand. On the contrary, he ought to help his colleagues who needed something from the big city. However, after accepting the mission, he felt a bit uncomfortable, as if wearing a pair of shoes which did not quite fit or a pair of trousers with different coloured legs.

His chief, noticing his hesitation, had phoned him several times since his arrival, urging him to see to this business. "Well, I'm not doing this for myself," he encouraged himself. And so he had come all this way and, covered with mud, had now reached his destination.

Luckily, he met two children who confirmed that this was the place he was looking for. He quickly climbed to the fourth floor, found the flat door, and, having calmed down, knocked gently yet loudly enough to be heard.

No response. After a while, there was a slight noise from inside. Chen listened, his ear against the door. Probably music. He was somewhat relieved, as it would have been disappointing not to find the man. He knocked loudly at the door again.

After the third knock, there came the sound of steps and then the turning of a lock. The door was opened to reveal a young man with a mop of unkempt hair, in a pair of underpants and flipflops. The lines of his body with its bulging muscles gleamed white. "Who are you looking for?" he asked impatiently.

"Comrade X," Chen stated the name on the envelope.

"He's not in." The young man turned to close the door.

Chen stepped forward and, trying to speak in the standard city accent, introduced himself and then asked, "Perhaps you're his relative? May I leave a message?"

It was quite dark in the doorway, and Chen could not make out his features clearly. However, he felt instinctively that the young man frowned. After a momentary hesitation, he said, "Come in then." With that, he turned to go in, like a nurse leading a patient in to see the dentist.

Chen followed him in. It was quiet except for their steps. They passed more doors than Chen had ever seen before in one flat. As one of them was pushed open by the young man, Chen was assailed by the smell of liquor.

Inside, the lamplight was soft. On the bed lay a crumpled silk-covered quilt. There was a fashionable, shining floor lamp. The door of a bedside locker was ajar revealing a new sophisticated lock, just the kind many of Chen's friends had asked him to buy, but which he had not seen in any store. Then he shifted his eyes to the rattan chairs, chaise-longue and a round table. A stereo tape-recorder from abroad was playing a song, by a Hong Kong singer, soft, clear and sentimental. It sounded ridiculous. If this was played in his little town, people would be scared stiff. The only familiar object in the room was a half-filled glass on the locker, like a friend in a strange place.

Chen spotted a rickety square stool by the door and, pulling it over, sat down despite his dirty clothes. He began to explain why he was there. After two sentences, he paused, hoping the man would take the hint and turn down the volume of the recorder. As he failed to do this, Chen had to carry on. He found it difficult to express himself and could only stammer incoherently, unable to find the right words. Instead of "Please tell Comrade X to arrange this," he said, "Could you do me a favour?" as though he wanted to borrow money. When he should have said, "I've come to make contact with you," he said humbly, "I need your help." Even the voice was not like his, but like a blunt saw on wood.

Then he produced the letter, but the young man did not stand up from his chaise-longue to take it. Though much older than he, Chen had to go over and hand it to him, getting a closer look at the pimply face, which wore an impatient, ignorant, conceited expression.

The young man flicked open the letter, glanced at it and smiled contemptuously, his left foot beating time to the music. Both the tape-recorder and the Hong Kong song were new to Chen. Though he did not exactly dislike the singing, he did not admire it. Unconsciously, a frown flitted across his face.

"Is this boss of yours really my father's old comrade-in-arms? I've never heard of him."

Chen felt insulted. Unable to check his anger, he retorted, "You're too young! Your father may not have mentioned him to you."

"My father says everyone who needs his car repaired claims to be his old army buddy."

Chen's face grew burning hot, his heart beat faster and beads of sweat stood on his forehead. "What do you mean? He went to Yan'an in 1936! His elder brother is the commander of C — military region!"

Chen was in such a fluster when mentioning that

commander, he suddenly felt dizzy and perspired profusely.

But all he got was a sneer, even more contemptuous.

Chen lowered his head, utterly ashamed of himself.

"Let me put it this way," the young man said, standing up as if about to make a report. "Nowadays, you've got to have two things to clinch a deal. First, goods. What can you give us in return?"

"Goods?" Chen asked himself. "What do we have? Legs of mutton?" he muttered as if talking to himself.

"That won't do!" The young man smiled again. His contempt had turned into pity. "Secondly, to be frank, you need to know a trick or two. . . . Why do you have to see my father? So long as you have goods and someone able, you can put through the deal in anyone's name." After a brief pause, he added, "My father's away at the seaside on business." He avoided saying "convalescing".

Chen's head was swimming. As he got to the door, he suddenly cocked his ears, for the recorder was now playing a familiar Hungarian classical waltz. It was good music. He imagined a leaf dancing over an azure lake surrounded on three sides by snow-capped mountains. And his hometown was on the other side of one of them. A wild goose alighted on the water.

Chen, as though drunk, rushed down the dark stairs. He heard something thumping but could not tell whether it was his heart or footsteps. He left the building and looked up. The pale orange-coloured lamp on the slanting pole had turned scarlet like a monster's eye!

What a frightening eye! Chen dashed forward, easily jumping over the ditch. The football match must have ended, for there was the announcer's bland voice reading the weather forecast. He hurried to the bus terminal, where many people were waiting. Some young women workers, apparently on night shift, were animatedly discussing the bonus system at their place of work. A young couple were talking intimately, arms round each other. Having got on the bus, Chen stood close to the door. This conductress was no longer young. She was very thin and her sharp shoulder-blades showed through her blouse. During the past twenty hard years, Chen had learned a lot at the expense of certain things to which he should have been entitled. However, he still loved lamplight, night-shift workers, democracy, bonus systems, legs of mutton. . . . The bus bell went and the three doors closed one after another. Outside, the shadows of trees and lamps began to recede. "Fares, please!" called the conductress. But before Chen could fish out his money, she had switched off her light, thinking all the passengers were night-shift workers.

Translated by Wang Mingjie

The Barber's Tale

FOR thirty years since 1949 I've been a barber in the Party's provincial committee's No. 1 Guest House. I was seventeen when New China was born and I started my apprenticeship.

Surrounded by glittering mirrors and fluorescent lamps, the fragrance of brilliantine, shampoo, toilet water and face cream, the sounds of scissors, clippers, hair driers and running water, I passed thirty years without even realizing it. Life seemed simple, uneventful yet happy. As I look back over the years, remorse, satisfaction and bewilderment overcome me.

My tiny barber's shop was also a reflection of the vicissitudes of life, especially since most of my customers were people of importance. During the first seven or eight years after Liberation, life was wonderful. All who came for a haircut and shave were comrades or army pals, very friendly to each other. One day, the other barber Xiao Wang was sick. While many customers were waiting their turn, a tall man in an army overcoat came over and addressed me as "Master" as he would a qualified barber. This made me blush for I was only twenty. Pointing at the vacant chair he asked, "May I help? I know something about haircutting." Then he turned to the customers, saying, "Which brave man dares to take a risk?"

A fat man in a grey uniform stood up. "I'm at your mercy."

The tall man proved extremely good. Later, I learned that he was the newly-appointed commander of the military area, while the fat one was a vice-minister. I came to know more people in leading positions as time went on. Secretary Zhang encouraged me to join the Party. Political Commissar Li bought me some ointment when I had an eye infection. Provincial Governor Zhao cleaned our wash basins and Department Head Liu repaired our broom while he was waiting his turn. Sometimes lower cadres and ordinary citizens, looking for these people, traced them to our shop. Several Young Pioneers and their instructor, a girl with two long plaits who spoke rapidly like a machine-gun, came once to look for the first secretary of the Party's provincial committee to beg him to take part in their Children's Day activities on June 1. They finally talked him round and made him promise to go.

In those years, leaders were close to the people. I fell in love with the new society, the revolution, and esteemed the international Communist leaders whose portraits we carried in the May Day parades. I deeply loved Marx, Mao Zedong and the Party leaders in my province and I believed in every word printed in the *People's Daily*, the provincial paper, the reports of the Party branch and our statutes and laws.

In the late fifties we celebrated the construction of new factories, electric power stations, bridges and the victory of the socialist reformation. But at the same time many unusual things happened. One day we'd hear that a certain high-ranking person was a wolf in sheep's clothing; the next that one-fourth of China's arable land would be growing flowers. Or that China would realize communism very soon. Incredible announcements, inferences and deeds were all too frequent. Though we were often shocked and amazed, we were nevertheless excited and encouraged and threw ourselves into our work. We felt that we were advancing, overcoming one difficulty after another. We were bold, full of enthusiasm and spared neither labour nor money.

During this period, some of my old customers disappeared. People whispered that they were in trouble. Those who came frowned, sighed and looked serious, the muscles on their faces taut. As they became busier and busier, no one had time for a barber like me. Not knowing what exactly were the problems of those customers who never came any more, nor being in a position to find out, I still had to join in denouncing them in political study sessions.

When the "cultural revolution" started, quite a few of my regular customers were severely criticized and persecuted — "bombarded" or "smashed", to use the jargon of the time. When the guest house was taken over by the so-called Leftists, the barber's was turned into their headquarters, with loudspeakers and machine-guns. It was often attacked by other Leftist factions. Though I didn't work, I collected my monthly salary just the same. I felt like a thief, taking money from a wallet I had picked up in the street.

In 1974, a "new revolutionary political power" was set up, the headquarters was transformed again into the barber's. It was littered with fragments of mirrors, fluorescent lamps, bullet shells, spears and clubs. We cleaned up the place and spent a large sum of money restoring it. That took four months. When iron railings were constructed around our guest house, two guards posted at the gate, and the hotel renamed the Worker-Peasant Guest House, real workers and peasants no longer had access to it. Special rooms with better beds and bathrooms and special food were prepared for the provincial and army leaders who had replaced those "capitalist roaders". But the quantity and quality of meals for ordinary guests went down. The new VIPs who came to my shop never condescended to give me a smile, to say nothing of bringing me eye drops or helping to repair a broom. . . . People's ways and morality had changed. Lonely and unhappy, I felt lost.

In the summer of 1975, a couple moved in. The man, in his fifties, was going grey. He had a large head and full lips. His eyes were lively and he always wore a half smile, which was both proud and sad. His wife was a small woman, tidy, trim and quick in her movements, but her face with its large eyes was devoid of all expression as if chiselled out of stone. They moved in with their belongings to a room in the corner of the top floor, the sixth floor, which had once been used as a storeroom, because there was no sunlight. They went to the dining room only when most people had left and the waiters had begun clearing up. Then they would eat whatever was still available. They never spoke to anyone and, apart from a young man in overalls who came to see them every Saturday evening, they had no visitors. Every morning at dawn the man came downstairs to do exercises under a big silk tree and then take a little walk. In the evenings he and his wife would stroll for exactly one hour and ten minutes. Other than that, they shut themselves in their room. A few times

I heard the man's loud, resonant laugh. Although the lift was often unoccupied and the girl operator smiled at them, they never used it. That made a very good impression on me, perhaps because few of those then in positions of power ever troubled to use their legs.

That morning I went as usual to the backyard to stretch my legs before work. The man was not there. Under the big silk tree, I began my Chinese boxing exercises, lifting my right heel, stepping forward, breathing deeply, bending my right knee and stretching the left one, when I suddenly heard a soft groan, as if someone was being throttled. The sound made my hair stand on end. Following it, I skirted a fountain, made my way through a row of cedars and saw a man prone on the ground outside the boiler room. I ran over. It was him. His face was bleeding, his upper lip gashed and the blood at his mouth was clogged with coal dust. I helped him up, but he was so weak that I had to carry him on my back to the drivers' office. The driver on duty was still dozing. I said to him, "This man's been injured or is ill. Take him to the hospital, quick."

Xiao Bu was the son of one of my colleagues, a young man whose hair and shoes shone, his shirt and pants always well-pressed. He examined the man, shook his head and said, "He's a counter-revolutionary. Don't bother about him."

"A counter-revolutionary?" I was startled, but the man's helpless and pitiable state touched me. "Nonsense! A counter-revolutionary wouldn't be staying here."

"Don't you know? He's Tang Jiuyuan!"

So that was him! In 1967, in all the streets, on pillars in restaurants and walls of public latrines, slogans written in tar, whitewash and paint read "Resolutely suppress... !" "Exercise dictatorship over... !" "Send ... to his doom!" and "Smash the head of that dog... !" with Tang Jiuyuan's name written upside-down or crooked. Three red crosses over his name meant that he deserved to be condemned to death. Opposing factions, fighting over our guest house and killing each other while striving to be the most "revolutionary", printed leaflets with pictures denouncing Tang as the Machiavelli behind the other faction. In 1970, it was officially announced that Tang had been sentenced to fifteen years in jail, his crime being that he had attacked the Central Cultural Revolution Group.* Now, this man, his eyes closed, groaning and bleeding, was in my arms.

The blood, groaning, limp body, pale face and closed eyes brought back to my mind his bright eyes, which were both melancholy and proud, and his unobtrusive behaviour. For some reason, I became agitated. "You've got to help a dying man! Even a counter-revolutionary must go to hospital in an emergency. You idiot! If anything happens to him, you'll be held responsible!"

Xiao Bu was the sort of youngster who'd argue with his own father. But now, gaping at me, he muttered, "Well, what... ?"

"Blame me. I'll use the car. I'll take the responsibility. Don't just stand there like a fool! Get the car started!"

Even now I cannot explain why I was so sympathetic to a "counter-revolutionary" who was a total stranger.

---

* An organization in the hands of Jiang Qing and Zhang Chunqiao.

Sometimes a thing has the opposite effect of that intended. When, in the past, indiscriminate emphasis was placed on drawing a clear line between classes, the line vanished; when struggling against each other was stressed, people realized the value of friendship and loyalty; when politics was over-emphasized, people became tired of it; and after the movement to sweep away all old ideas, customs and habits, people clung to these things even more.

We took Tang to the hospital in a jeep. He was ill with Ménière's disease and had become dizzy and fainted, cutting his lips. The doctor stitched up his wound and then he was hospitalized for slight concussion. A few days later he was well enough to be discharged.

One evening, Tang and his wife dressed themselves up and came to my shop, inviting me to dinner to show their gratitude. They opened many tins of expensive food, prawns, Beijing duck, fungus, mushrooms and so on. Unable to buy things which were difficult to get in the market, they spent a lot of money on tinned food. After a few cups of wine, Tang began to talk in his resonant voice. And he was a good talker!

"I'm fifty-four this year. In 1938 I joined the Eighth Route Army. I was just seventeen. I was the regimental commander of an artillery unit in 1949. After being demobbed, I was the Party secretary of N Prefecture for more than seventeen years. I thought I'd be there for life. But in 1967 I was thrown into prison for eight years. . . ."

His indignant wife butted in, "He was shut up with high Kuomintang officials. When I took his meals to him, their wives looked at me with such hatred. . . ."

A chill went down my spine.

"Come on, help yourself. We've nothing good to offer you now. But some day I'll give you a really good meal to thank you properly," said Tang.

"He would have died if you hadn't helped him, Old Lu. The driver didn't want to take him. Such people are so short-sighted! One day...."

"Now, now, enough of that," Tang insisted, changing the topic. "When I was in solitary confinement, before I was thrown into jail, I nearly kicked the bucket. I was put in a room by myself, since I was an 'important criminal!'. The room was fairly warm. But the young man who guarded me felt that a counter-revolutionary mustn't be too comfortable, so he broke my door panel with a rifle butt. The piercing wind blew in, and I got pneumonia. They debated heatedly about whether or not I should be sent to hospital. My guard didn't want to waste penicillin on a counter-revolutionary. Thank goodness one of his leaders stuck to our humane policy ...."

He was a tough man, telling such a horrible story casually and sprinkling it with humour.

But his wife hissed, "You're an old comrade too, Old Lu. Tell me, what's going on? We fought to liberate the country and build New China and we are now being persecuted by landlords, bad elements and counter-revolutionaries. I call this class vengeance!"

Tang downed a few more cups of wine. When I tried to stop him, his wife said, "He never lets himself go. Let him drink so that he doesn't bottle everything up inside him."

With tear-filled eyes, Tang continued, "I didn't waste the eight years I was shut up. I went back over my life and analysed myself. It was better than spending a few years in the Party school. I recalled all I'd done since I joined the revolution, especially when I was the secretary of the Party's prefectural committee. I reviewed every one of my successes and mistakes. Great wrongs had been done to me, but hadn't ever wronged anybody? I was framed, but hadn't I blamed people unjustly when I was in power? Why are prisoners maltreated? Even if they are real counter-revolutionaries, they should be justly dealt with according to the law. Why insult and persecute them unlawfully? How had my young guard become so ultra-Left, ignoring policies and the law? We were to blame!" He banged his fist on the table and cried in a hoarse voice, "Time and again I've told myself, if ever I'm cleared and resume work, first, I'll be very careful when dealing with people. Second, I'll improve the conditions in the prison and guarantee that the prisoners get proper treatment. Third, I'll never promote or rely on any ultra-Leftists!"

My heart, contracted and numbed by the many sudden changes and the unfathomable savagery of the world around me, revived a little with his sincere and frank words, like rain moistening the parched, cracked earth. Tears coursed down my face though what he had said had nothing to do with me. For years, the bragging in the newspapers, on the radio or TV, on the stage and in meeting rooms had jarred on my ears. When I heard this sensible talk from the former Party secretary, I knew that not all the good people had died. Faith, sincerity, seeking truth from facts and reason, all of which had been buried for a long time, still remained. How could I check my tears?

We became great friends. Friendship gave warmth to

my lonely heart. Awake at midnight, I was happy to know that I had a respected friend, in whom I could confide and whom I could support and protect for the time being. After that my existence had more meaning. I wanted to do all I could for Old Tang to make his life easier. I had some connections with grocers and salesmen and could often get him things which were rare in the market like cucumbers in May, famous wines and live carp. Since my son worked in a bookstore I got him hard-to-get books too. During the Spring Festival, I invited him and his wife over for a meal of dumplings, pork stewed with distillers' grain, and preserved eggs. My son set off fireworks. When I built a little storeroom in the backyard his son, the young man in overalls, came to help and became friends with my son. They went swimming, learned to play the guitar together and lent each other banned books....

"Old Lu, do Provincial Secretary Zhao and his family have their hair done at your place? When he comes again, will you let me know? I want to have a word with him," Old Tang said to me one night.

"Talk to him?" I was amazed. It was no secret that Zhao was a notorious careerist, who went along with the new mandarins.

Mrs Tang twisted her mouth disdainfully. "Talk to him indeed! Who do you think he is?"

"What else can I do? Keep on doing nothing just because I was framed? He represents the Party at his level." Turning to me he said, "I was accused of attacking the Central Cultural Revolution Group. I'd never have dared to do that. I've never attacked anybody. It was a complete frame-up. I don't even know what I was supposed to have said or done! But a Communist must work for the Party...."

"Oh, forget it. It sounds marvellous — work for the Party!" His wife was in a rage. "All you want is an official post, that's all. What's so special about a leading post? The Organization Department talked to me today, appointing me deputy-secretary of a factory. I went straight to the hospital and got myself sick leave for three months. I worked for the revolution all my life. Then I was persecuted for eight long years.... Now I'm given such a low official post."

As we were intimate friends, his wife's outburst didn't embarrass Tang, who explained to me, "It's wrong to view things in this light. A Party member should be able to stand trials. Besides, I have a son and a married daughter. My grandchildren aren't allowed to become Red Guards because of me. How can I sit still and not look up Secretary Zhao?"

I had heard many such arguments and knew that Mrs Tang was not happy with her post. She had mentioned before that, according to her rank before the "cultural revolution", she ought to be the vice-director of the light industry bureau at the very least. She had also said that since Old Tang was still under a cloud, she could not get a suitable job. Although people who had never been in leading positions were not familiar with this kind of thinking, I didn't find it too odd, for they were her honest thoughts. Even a barber or his apprentice could imagine the discontent of a leading cadre demoted from a high position in a bureau to a lowly one in a small factory. I was at first disgusted with the importance some people placed on official posts, but I soon realized that many charlatans and thugs had climbed up in the world by treading on others. Why should veterans like the Tangs be expected to accept demotion and be satisfied with a low post, while those scoundrels threw their weight about? After all, the Tangs had done valuable work for the revolution, and during the "cultural revolution" they had reviewed their past work and become wiser. Moreover, I was a supporter of his three-point platform. If he was not in a leading post how could he carry it out? His concern over the future of his grandchildren called for sympathy too. So I pinned my hopes for the future of our country, Party and myself on old comrades like him.

Breaking my rule of keeping my nose out of everything, I began to look for Secretary Zhao. I don't know how they finally met and talked. Anyway, soon the news came that Tang was to be the eighth deputy director of the supply and marketing co-op, much to the indignation of Mrs Tang. "Huh! A prefectural secretary put in such a position," she sneered. Old Tang smiled and said nothing, apparently just glad to work again. But the political atmosphere changed once more by the end of that year. The "gang of four" and their followers criticized the return of the old, disgraced cadres. So Tang was unable to take up even that small post.

In January 1976, Old Tang, his wife and I mourned deeply the loss of Premier Zhou. They went to the People's Square with the masses. Tang told me agitatedly, "It's more than mourning. It's a political demonstration!" His eyes burned with the fury of the former artillery commander. I felt that he was planning a battle. We discussed affairs of state with great concern, but he clammed up after the Tiananmen Incident was declared a counter-revolutionary act on April 7. He warned me when I sometimes let off steam, "You must be careful! This is a serious matter!" I was disappointed and bewildered, but knowing his situation I understood how he felt.

In October 1976, the "gang of four" was overthrown. The following February, Secretary Zhao was transferred, owing to his connection with the gang. The committee was reshuffled. In March, the Party's new provincial committee called a big meeting to reinstate Old Tang. The news media claimed that he had been persecuted for opposing the gang and that he had withstood the test. He was compared to a lofty pine, battling against snowstorms. A week later, Tang was appointed secretary of the Party committee of S city, a municipality directly under the province. As he was busy, I didn't go to see him but drank his health with my family. Before he left for his new post he, his wife and son came to say goodbye, inviting us to visit them. Old Tang assured me that if I ever needed help, I could count on him. He wanted to stay and talk, but his wife, who was happy now, reminded him that a certain political commissar was giving them a farewell dinner. He held my hand tightly when the car started, begging me again to visit him. I was very touched. But one thing marred the occasion. As soon as they had walked in, my son left on some excuse and didn't turn up again until bedtime. When I questioned him about it, he said between his clenched teeth, "Don't befriend the high and mighty!"

Furiously, I reproved him, "That's no way to talk! We're comrades and friends, whatever his situation, I'll never ass-lick just because he's a high official. You know your father. But I can't give him the cold shoulder either." My son smiled nonchalantly. That was how he always reacted whenever I tried to lecture him. Feeling insulted, I demanded in a loud voice, "What are you smiling at?"

Avoiding my eyes, he replied in a tired voice, "I feel you're so naive!" Imagine a son calling his father naive! "Did he really fight hard against the gang? Was he really so lofty? Did he have the correct attitude towards working at a lower post?"

Stumped by his questions, I flared up at once. "You've no class feeling! The gang persecuted old comrades, and now you try to find fault with them. It's dangerous if you go on like this!"

My son turned away. Despondently, I thought to myself, the arguments and ways of reasoning which had proved extremely effective, moving and powerful with my generation didn't wash with my son's.

New Year, 1978. Old Tang wrote and sent me a parcel of crisp sweets flavoured with cassia, a speciality of S city, and invited my family to visit them again. I couldn't make up my mind. A busy man's time was precious. My wife urged me to go, while my son protested, "You mean to go? Don't forget, he's the municipal secretary."

My head drooped. But did a distance between our positions necessarily mean a distance between our two honest hearts? I couldn't believe it.

My mind made up, I asked my wife to prepare some of Old Tang's favourite dishes. Two days before the Spring Festival, the day before I planned to leave, Xiao Bu, the driver, called. He brought a box of cakes and two bottles of wine and chatted away. He offered to place his car at my disposal whenever it was needed. Then he remarked, "Your table would look much better if it had a plastic cover. I've one just about the right size. You can have it. Your bicycle needs to be re-chromed. I'll have it done for you."

As we had never had much to do with each other, I wondered why he had called. After beating about the bush for a long time, he finally came to the point. "I admire you, Old Lu. An older man has more experience. You have foresight. By looking after Old Tang while he was in difficulty, you made a useful friend. But you and I are just ordinary blokes. I'm twenty-eight and still a bachelor but at last I've found a girl friend. To tell you the truth, she's a doll! She doesn't demand a wardrobe or a TV set. She only wants to be transferred from the suburbs to the centre and have her work changed from weaving to spinning. So I've come to ask you a favour. I heard that you're going to S city to-morrow." He pushed the cakes and wine to me.

"I . . . what can I do?" I was perplexed.

"That depends on you. Old Tang's your friend. You've done him many good turns."

I flushed. "What . . . are you talking about?"

He was going to press his point when my son came over, handed him back the cakes and wine and firmly showed him the door. "Go and ask somebody else. My father isn't going there."

"You can't do that to me. You may need me some day. . . ."

Shutting the door, my son shot me a reproachful look.

I let out a deep sigh and told my wife, "Better cancel my ticket!"

June that year, the financial and commercial bureaux

called a conference in the provincial city to learn from Daqing and Dazhai, the models in industry and agriculture at that time. I attended and had the opportunity to meet the representatives from S city. I took pains to find out what they thought of Tang.

Although newspapers and documents had stressed many times that inside the Party we should address each other as comrades, most people still called their leaders by their titles. "Secretary Tang has done well. The city's clean and tidy. He's set up traffic regulations, planted trees... and investigated what the followers of the 'gang of four' did. He has guts."

They told me an anecdote to show how strict Tang was. He had gone to investigate a grocery during the Spring Festival without revealing his identity. The manager sold large quantities of rationed food to his friends and wouldn't admit his mistake when it was pointed out. Tang had criticized him severely. It was like a story about a just official in history. My heart rejoiced at what I heard, as if I had something to do with it.

"Did he improve the conditions in your prison?" I inquired. No one answered. They all looked at me strangely. Asking or replying to such a question was suspicious. I smiled wryly. "Is there anything against him?" I asked again.

"Well. His wife's a bitch, lashing out at her inferiors and superiors. She scolds everyone. I'm scared to death as soon as she walks into my store!"

"He's exaggerating," another piped up. "She's hot-tempered, that's all. If you rub her the right way, she's all right."

But others had different views. "They live in a luxurious flat. Their son isn't married, but he's got another big flat. Their daughter's being transferred to our city from another town. Mrs Tang's also applying for a flat for her and her husband."

We spoke in low voices. Although the room wasn't bugged, people naturally whispered when talking about their superiors.

Their complaints gave me food for thought and kept me awake that night. What was wrong with her? They had suffered and people had sympathized with them. If she thought only of making up for their losses caused by the "gang of four", this was not the way. People had put their trust in them. . . . If they should isolate themselves from the people. . . . It was unthinkable!

I felt the urge to go to S city, to see Old Tang and his wife and tell them what I had heard. Now that they were high officials, not many people would speak honestly and openly to them. I was on tenterhooks until the conference ended. The last two days were set aside for the representatives to go sightseeing, see some shows, have banquets and take photos. I gave up these and asked for leave to visit Old Tang.

It took me four hours by overnight train. On my arrival, I was eating my breakfast in a restaurant when I came across one of my former fellow apprentices, whom I had not seen for years. Surprise was clearly written on his face when he learned that I had come to see Old Tang.

"You've come to complain to Secretary Tang? I always thought you were a cautious character. Never went looking for trouble."

"But, we know each other. He asked me to visit him."

"Visit?" His eyes popped. Then he seemed to see the light. "Good for you. It never occurred to me that a simple man like you had learned the necessity of having connections with important persons. Well, well. That's the style!" He stuck up his thumb. Then he whispered to me, "Tomorrow, the provincial committee is calling a work conference in this city. The best chefs and performers have all been told to report and rare goods in the city have been commandeered for the conference. Even the cold-drinks stores are closing. You must stay in the hotel for VIPs. If you see any good buys, please think of me. Have you brought enough money? My home's not far away. . . ."

My uneasiness increased. Without stopping to rest or find a room, I hurried to the office of the Party's provincial committee and was told that Tang was at the No. 1 Guest House, the VIP hotel. Two hundred metres from the gate, I caught sight of a policeman and a soldier on duty, who were there specially for the conference. Fifty metres from the gate they questioned me. "Where're you going?" They didn't even say comrade. Then I had to show my identity card, before I was allowed to approach the gate.

I was told to go to the gate house which was closed, its windows screened with white paper, to prevent outsiders from looking in. How could I get admission? On the other side of the gate house, a small window was open. Those who wanted admittance were grilled first.

The small window was very high, as if for basketball players over two metres tall. A board shut off one-third of it. On tiptoe, I stretched my neck and shouted,

"Comrade!" My neck ached. I saw only the back of a burly man.

"Comrade! Comrade!" I shouted several times before he half-turned his head, threw me a glance and then turned back again.

"Comrade!" I yelled.

"Can't you speak?" His question hit me like a bullet.

Speak? I was not dumb. I spoke Chinese. My face fell and turned scarlet.

"I want to see Old Tang. I want to see Tang Jiu-yuan."

The soldier cried, "Don't shout!"

The name and the way I uttered it had borne weight. The gateman turned around, moved forward and looked me up and down, giving me the shivers. I'd rather face an enemy than the scrutiny of this comrade. Then he began to ask questions. When he knew who I was, he said coldly, "No guests are received during the conference."

"But it doesn't start until tomorrow. The Party committee sent me here."

"No guests!" he mumbled and showed me his back again. Then at the sound of a woman's voice he leapt to the door, a different man. The voice had wrought a miraculous change over him as if a Bodhisattva had sprinkled him with some magic water. Charming and warm, he turned the lock and opened the door.

"A few of my son's friends are coming to see the film tonight. Please admit them." It was the voice of Mrs Tang.

"Certainly. No problem. I know Young Tang. When he comes with them. . . ."

"They might not come together."

"That's all right! Tell them to mention Young Tang. . . ." I was amazed at how obedient and affable he could be.

"But he won't let *me* in!" I protested. Mrs Tang's voice had made me bolder.

"Oh, Old Lu? What a pleasure to see you!" Mrs Tang greeted me. At a wave of her hand the gateman, all smiles, gave me a pass. His smile was more detestable than his sizing me up from head to toe. I quickly turned and entered the gate.

I complained to Mrs Tang about the manners of the gateman and the heavily-guarded entrance. "This VIP hotel of yours is too distinguished," I commented.

She laughed and retorted, "Cut it out! One can't get into your Worker-Peasant Guest House so easily either! What can we do? So many people come with their complaints. There'd be no work done if everyone were allowed in." Cordially she drew closer to me. "You're always in our thoughts. We hoped you'd join us for the Spring Festival. I told Old Tang you were our true friend and a good comrade. Now he's the Party secretary of the city so many people come to see him. Old colleagues, former subordinates, schoolmates, relatives — people who've had nothing to do with us for years! I wonder why they didn't show up before. When I was taking meals to Old Tang in the prison, none of them said a kind word to me." She was indignant.

I consoled her, "Things are different now."

She cheered up again. "Yes. Stay a few days. Don't go back in a hurry. I'll show you around. I'm careful not to work too hard now, so I can help you shop, or arrange for you to see a special doctor. Any medicine you want? What I can't do, Old Tang can. There's no problem." She was then interrupted and called away. As she left she told me, "Old Tang is in Courtyard No. 3. Go and see him." She added, "Stay here tonight. We're showing a foreign film."

I went in the direction she had pointed. Passing by a store, my attention was caught by an advertisement: Fur, wool, televisions, leather shoes — most sought-after commodities — sold at bargain prices! I frowned. There was also a cold-drinks kiosk. I walked in to get an ice lolly to cool myself down after the scene outside the gate-house. It was better and cheaper than what was available in the market. I'd never enjoyed such luxury in all the years I'd worked in the big guest house in the provincial city. The ice lolly chilled my mouth and stomach. Then the cold spread to my heart.

"I must talk to Old Tang. Why should a conference have so many perks? People will talk no matter how carefully they guard the gates. I must ask him how he's going on with his three-point platform." I came to the No. 3 courtyard where there were a few cars including a Red Flag, a Datsun and a Mercedes Benz, apparently belonging to high officials. A happy Old Tang was directing them like a capable traffic policeman to a cool, breezy shaded place near the gate. In a new good-quality suit, which showed the edge of the starched collar of his very white shirt, he shook hands with every driver and told the attendants to take them to their quarters. When he turned around, his eyes fell on me.

I was on the point of greeting him, when a bespectacled man came over and handed him a document.

While reading the document Old Tang said to another, "Check the bath tubs of No. 1 courtyard again. The attendants are too lazy! When I inspected them yesterday, my hands got dirty. The showers didn't work properly either. I gave those boys a talking-to. . . ."

More people came over. Old Tang told them one by one:

"You go and check the auditorium."

"You look over the kitchen. They must get some vinegar from Shanxi."

"You check the store."

"You go to the clinic. . . ."

"Publish a bulletin two or three times a day. What? You've nothing to write? Well. For today you can say something like, 'The people of our city are most honoured to have the conference held here.' You don't want me to teach you that, do you?"

"Tell him he must attend. This conference comes before everything else. Tell him I expect to see him here."

"We'll look into that later. Tell him to wait. I spent eight years in prison. What's his hurry?"

"No. I'm too busy. Tell them to go to the education bureau."

After these people had left, others came with more documents and questions. All were honoured to have a few words with Secretary Tang.

Half an hour passed and then an hour. The people around him finally dispersed. Exhausted, he turned to leave.

I addressed him, "Old Tang."

He turned to me. Overcome with fatigue, he looked at me vaguely. Suddenly his eyes lit up. "Why, it's Old Xu. So you've arrived?" He walked over and took my hand listlessly.

I looked at him sadly. There was a hint of reproach in my voice when I said, "You don't remember me?"

"Sorry. Old Li. No. You're Old Lu. I'm really getting on," he complained and lowered his head. He had more lines on his forehead and more grey hairs.

"How are you? Do you still have your dizzy spells?"

"Oh, I'm all right. Only too busy. Much too busy. Can't get anything done."

Several older men came out. The most distinguished one, dressed in a grey jacket, which was undone, had on a pair of Chinese cloth shoes. In an even voice with a southern accent he asked, "Hi, Old Tang! Will you join us for a walk?"

They were the leading cadres of the province. Old Tang gave me a brief handshake, urged me to stay for a few days and turned away. I stepped nearer, as if afraid of losing him. "But I want to have a word with you, Old Tang." My voice quivered. He turned and looked at me with concern.

"Your store. . . ." Before I could finish, he beckoned to a young man and told him, "Give him two ration cards and find him a room."

He left. I almost collapsed. As the young man reached out to help me, I pushed him away and shambled off.

Back home, I told my friends about my experiences. Many of them criticized me arguing, "You shouldn't have left like that. He's old and busy. You should have waited until he had the time to talk to you." But my son, the rotter, said only three words, "Serves you right!"

During last year's Spring Festival, Old Tang and his wife again sent me a letter and a package of preserved fruit. My name was written correctly on the envelope. He again invited my family to visit him, regretting that we couldn't be together the last time. It was in Old Tang's handwriting. I was very touched by his sincerity and warmth, treating me like his equal. I blamed myself for the unpleasantness caused by the last visit. I had been too impatient, too subjective. Old Tang could not be blamed for being so busy. And there was nothing wrong about looking after the drivers of his superiors. His wife's bad temper was not his fault either. All in all, what I had against him was only the low price of the various goods and the ice lollies, one of which I'd eaten myself! The Central Party Committee had been issuing many documents on this problem and commissions for inspecting discipline had been set up at various levels. So I presumed they wouldn't do that any more. What society could do away with its officials? Who should be the officials? I was opposed to Zhao and those rebel commanders who bashed down all officials. I myself had neither the ability nor the wish to be one. Since I supported Old Tang, why be so hard on him? I should allow him time to carry out his three-point platform. I shouldn't persecute officials like the rebel commanders, nor should I make use of them like Bu the driver and my fellow apprentice. I would neither fawn on them nor avoid them like my son, nor be antagonistic. Too much blood had been shed. Many lives were sacrificed overthrowing the Kuomintang and the "gang of four" and their followers. Our old comrades were once again in power and running things. If everyone avoided them, not telling them what he thought, what would happen to our country and the Party? My tears fell. I made up my mind to make another trip to see Old Tang and his wife and take them some fine dishes cooked at home.

Translated by Yu Fanqin

Voices of Spring

NIGHT arrived with a screech. A faint square of moonlight appeared on the opposite wall. Yue Zhifeng tensed and then relaxed. The carriage swayed lightly. The people swayed lightly. A sweet cradle of youth! In summertime, leaving their clothes under the willow, his bare-bottomed young gang jumped into the clear stream at home, and one bold child dived down a dozen metres, no one knew whose head would poke up where. No one knew how many frogs and tadpoles were contained in the mouthful of water he swallowed in panic. When they closed their eyes and fell fast a-sleep in the rippling water flecked with sunlight and shade from the trees, they swayed lightly then as they swayed now. Youth and home that is lost and not lost, do you blame me? Will you welcome me? Mother's grave and father on his way to the grave?

The square of moonlight shifted, disappeared and was reborn again. A single small square window had let in this beam of light, was it the afterglow of the setting sun or the light from the station platform? It was pitch black, as if the fast gathering afternoon were already night. The door closed with a screech, closing off the outside world. Was it hail beginning to fall, this noise that became ever more insistent? Was it an iron hammer striking an iron anvil? Throughout this loess plateau country we still rely on people who forge iron, how mus-

cular are our country's arms! Ah, of course, it is only the
din of the wheels striking against the rails, coming
from the cracks between one section of the track and
the next. Isn't there a tender song popular just now
called what is it, *The Tinkle of the Fountain*? Can a
train be said to make a tinkling sound? Guangzhou people really know how to live, not like on this northwest
plateau where people's faces and the windowpanes are
all covered with a layer of thick dust. Guangzhou people hang many, many triangular porcelain tablets underneath their awnings, which catch the cool breezes
and make a clear tinkling sound very refreshing to the
spirits. But American *musique concrète* drives you out
of your mind. I wonder what Kissinger thinks when he
listens to our Yang Zirong arias? The drums and
gongs of Beijing opera create a great din. Is a din always displeasing? On the contrary, the sound of the
wheels when the train starts offers encouragement and
hope. At the next stop, or the stop after next, or the
stop after many more stops, is the new life you are seeking; a mother or child, a friend or wife, a hot tub or
a hearty dinner awaits you there. Everyone is going
home for the lunar New Year, the Spring Festival, the
favourite old Chinese festival of us all. Thank heavens
the whole country can now have a happy New Year. No
one can destroy the Spring Festival any more in the
name of "revolutionizing" it.

It was really curious. After returning from a three-
month tour abroad and staying for a spell at a high-
level hotel in Beijing — summarizing his experiences,
writing up his notes, being interviewed, making his reports — Yue Zhifeng received a letter from his father,
now in his eighties, who had just had his landlord "cap"

removed. He decided to make a return to his native district after a long separation of more than twenty years. Had it been a mistake? It had not occurred to him then that he would have to sit in a sealed boxcar for two hours and forty-seven minutes. Three hours earlier, he had been sitting on the wide comfortable seat of a Trident from Beijing to X city. Two months before, he had been sitting in a steamer on the Elbe heading for Hamburg. And now, he was squeezed against these travel-weary passengers, whose faces he could hardly distinguish in the darkness, packed together like sardines in a tin. He could not even tell in which direction the train was going. There was only the moonlight-like patch of light, shifting rapidly in and out of his gaze. Was it going in the same direction as the train or the opposite? This problem, to which even a primary school student could have answered, bothered this engineering physicist for quite a time.

He had not been back to his old home for more than twenty years. Whose fault was it that he had been born from the wrong womb? Landlord, landlord! He had gone back once in 1956, once was enough for loneliness — he only stayed at home four days, but his self-criticism lasted twenty-two years! What troubled him was that the purpose of life could surely not be self-criticism. Luckily, all of that was in the past. The assembly line in the Stuttgart Mercedes-Benz Factory moved without stopping, the workshop was immaculate and gleaming, and there was not much of a racket. Siemens was a large-scale enterprise with a history of a hundred and thirty years. We have just taken our first steps. Catch up, catch up, in spite of all the difficulties. *Mou, mou, mou,* hurry up now, hurry up now, hurry up, hurry up, hurry, hurry; the noise of the wheels changed from a low three beats per bar to two beats per bar and then into a loud resonant cry. Even the sealed boxcar was in a hurry. How much more so the Trident in the sky?

Amid the dust and cigarette fumes emerged the acrid smell of a pipe, which had an effect like acupuncture and moxibustion on the windpipe and lungs. A plum-blossom needle plunged right into a lobe of his lung. The smell of sweat was much milder. The thickness of the local dialect, between the tobacco smoke and the smell of sweat, was both irritating and intimate. And the smell of pumpkin! Who was eating pumpkin? He had not seen anyone selling cooked pumpkin in front of X railway station. Other kinds of snacks and local specialities, however, were all there. Peanuts, walnuts, sunflower seeds, dried persimmons, liquored dates, mung bean cakes, potatoes, castor beans ... were all for sale. Then just like a conjuring trick, a red cloth was raised, two fingers pointed to the left, and everything disappeared, even matches, batteries and soap becoming scarce. And now, it will soon change again, if you stretch out your hand to grab another handful or two, you might grab even more riches. Persimmons and dates are simple, natural products, but their sweetness goes right to people's hearts. Yue Zhifeng chewed on some dried persimmons he had bought before getting on the train, carefully savouring each burst of sweetness. Pungency produces an immediate sensation, but sweetness is deeply buried. One must be patient, serious, experienced, sensitive. Over the stench of the acrid tobacco and warm sweat, Yue Zhifeng smelled the scent of mung beans carried by the local people. Mung bean sprouts are delicious, and so are hares, but wild hares will destroy the beans. To catch wild hares, he and young Zhuzi raced for three *li* without pausing for breath, so fast that even the trees along the dikes swayed from side to side. On the night of the mid-autumn harvest moon, he saw with his own eyes a silver fox silently crossing the road, like a fairy, like a dream.

The noise from the train subsided, the noise from the train came to a stop. The noise from people increased, the noise from people reached a crescendo. Scree — ch, the iron door opened, and the train attendant — a tall girl, large-framed — was giving a stream of directions in the local dialect to the passengers getting off and on. "There's no room left, no room left, get on the next carriage," this ineffective and rather selfish cry issued from someone who had already secured his own place on the train. The embarking passengers crowded on, a swarming mass of activity. Wherever you go there is a swarming mass of activity. Compared with our Wangfujing Street, one could say that the streets of Hamburg were practically deserted, and also the population of the city was smaller. Yue Zhifeng had got a shock when he arrived at X Station from the airport — a dense mass of heads, the trampled white snow no longer white, the ilex no longer green. Had there been some kind of incident? There had not been so many people even at the time of the 1946 student movement, when everyone had gathered in the station square to block the train to Nanjing and present a petition! When Yue Zhifeng was at university in Beijing, he once went for a stroll around the Palace Museum. It was four in the afternoon, but there was not a soul in sight, and the gloomy great halls had sent shivers up and down his spine. He left the palace at a slight run, and only relaxed when he got on the crowded trolley-bus. If he had gone more slowly, Princess Zhen might have whirled up from her well and pushed him in! But now there are long lines of people buying tickets at the south and north gates of the Palace Museum. And it wasn't a Sunday. The crowd in front of X Station made one's head spin. It was as if half of China wanted to get on the train on the eve of the Spring Festival. There were reunions and parties everywhere, dumpling parties and glutinous rice dumpling parties, for old friends and for partings, the joys of family reunions and the search for home and childhood. The man selling meat dumplings had just taken off his shoes, and the white sheet covering the dumplings was filthy all over. People selling sesame buns, flat cakes, crullers, pancakes. People selling whole boxes of pastries. People selling bread and biscuits. The catering services at X Station and X city had thrown all their resources into the open air market in front of the station. You had to push until you sweated even to buy a couple of sesame cakes. Yue Zhifeng was pouring with sweat! Recklessly stuffing himself (the swift change in his environment and material conditions had made him unable to distinguish hunger and fullness), he then bought a ticket on a short-distance passenger train to his home village. When he handed over the money he became alarmed, the price listed was one yuan twenty, why did they only take sixty cents? Hadn't he pronounced distinctly the name of his station? He thought of asking again, but the person standing in line behind him had already occupied the favoured position in front of the ticket window and he couldn't push his way back. Morosely he looked at the ticket in his hand. On the ticket was printed 1.20 yuan in black letterpress, but it was crossed out by two large words written in double lines occupying the whole surface of the ticket: sixty cents. This left him puzzled and perplexed, it was just like a biological code. "What's this? Why did she give me a sixty-cent ticket when I asked for one yuan twenty?" he said to himself. He asked others. No one answered. People waiting for a train are mostly egoists who can be excused on the grounds of being already fully occupied.

Assorted items of information dashed around in his brain. The dense mass of people. The filthy cotton sheet over the steaming hot dumplings. The announcement in large print pasted up in the waiting room: the situation concerning additional train services for the Spring Festival period and the timetable for temporary additional services. The long queues of people in front of the men's and women's toilets waiting to have a pee. The words sixty cents in double lines. The big parcels and little parcels, big baskets and little baskets, big bags and little bags. . . . He reached the conclusion that this last stretch of his journey might be difficult. He was being ideologically prepared. Finally when he heard the words "sealed boxcar" in conversation among the passengers he suddenly understood. The human brain is much cleverer after all than an electronic brain.

When it was time to get on the train, he was feeling somewhat depressed. On the eve of the first Spring Festival of the eighth decade of the twentieth century, people who passed their days and nights possessed of hopes of realizing the four modernizations still had to travel by a sealed boxcar dating from the time of Watt and Stephenson. Such is reality. Reality is like the universe, like the globe, Mount Hua and the Yellow

River, water and earth, hydrogen and oxygen, titanium and uranium. It is not as soft and gentle as imagination, nor as cruel and cold as imagination. And wasn't it so, the sealed boxcar was full of people, and yet still in ones and twos, in tens and twenties, moving into the cracks between people they embedded themselves in the spaces between one molecule and the next, one atom and the next. It was like a miracle that defied explanation how so many people were added to a carriage which was already full. No one grumbled.

Someone grumbled, "This box won't take any weight!" A woman wearing a scarf and carrying a child was trying to see if she could find a box to sit on. "Why don't you come over here? Over here." Yue Zhifeng promptly stood up and offered the place to the side that he had been occupying. This position where one could lean against the carriage wall was an excellent "private room". The woman was somewhat embarrassed. But in the end she moved over with the child, managing with a great deal of effort not to tread on the others. "Thank you so much," said the woman in an easy Beijing accent. She lifted her head. Yue Zhifeng visualized a charcoal sketch. It should be entitled "The Smile".

A bell rang tingling, the iron door closed again with a screech and an even deeper night descended. The twilight outside the train was also growing more opaque. The large-framed train attendant lit a white candle and put it on a square glass table. Why not use a kerosene lamp? They may have been afraid that the kerosene would spill. In a carriage as big as this, we depend on this one candle for light. Illuminated in the weak light the passengers turned into individual shadows. The carriage was swaying again, and the square patch of light on the opposite wall of the carriage was also shifting rapidly. They were getting nearer to his home village. His "cap" removed and seeing his son again, his father should be able to close his eyes in peace. His crimes and his repentance, his tears and gratitude, his wicked sins and his honest goodness would all disperse like a mist soon after his demise. One by one the older generation were on their way to the far side of the river. *Dong, dong, dong, deng, deng, deng, beng, beng, beng,* were they crossing a bridge? A bridge between the past and the future, China and the outside world, the city and the countryside, near bank and the far.

The candle which was standing very near her printed a pattern of clearly accentuated brightness and shadows on the train attendant's face. She resembled a full-length statue of a goddess. "Comrade travellers, during the Spring Festival, passenger transport is very crowded, our regular carriages are dispatched on the long-distance.... Enhance vigilance...." She spoke energetically, spitting out every word as if she were tightening a screw. She had an air of perfect confidence, an ability to direct people with ease; though young in years and relying on the light of a single candle, she exerted her leadership over a carriage of unruly passengers. But her voice was drowned in the *hong, hong, hong, weng, weng, weng, long, long, long,* that created such a terrible racket.

Free markets. Department stores. Hong Kong electronic quartz watches. The Henan opera *Juan Xi Tong.* Steamed buns in mutton soup. Fermented rice cakes. Three-piece leather shoes. Three-sided tile hats. Team-level production quotas. Green onions for sale. A Chinese medicine cancer cure. The elections. Wedding feasts.... In the midst of this animated chatter Yue Zhifeng shifted his body weight in turn from his left leg to his right and from his right leg to his left. It is fortunate that people have two legs, or it would be really unbearable to have to stand without any support in a dense press of people and things. Somewhere to stick an awl — Yue Zhifeng now had a vivid understanding of this common expression. Is it possible that they had such crowded carriages with no seats and no lights in ancient times? But he had offered a woman comrade his "seat". No, there were no seats, only places. He had not expected that she would have a Beijing accent. This seemed to heighten his interest. Polite expressions such as "thank you" and "excuse me" were common in other countries. Although there was a tightly packed sack containing iron machinery pressing on his calf. And the spine of someone sitting on a mat was leaning sharply against his left leg which had become uncomfortably numb.

It was quite incredible. Not only when he was watching a performance in a Munich theatre, but even in Beijing, in the research institute, in the ministry and in the hotel, in the 23 square metres room and the 103 and 332 bus routes, he had not expected that people were still being transported in sealed boxcars. Aren't they for goods and animals? Damn it! But damn what? Cursing is too easy. It's less effort and attracts more attention to curse a sealed boxcar than to build a fine new comfortable passenger train. The spittle of people who have nothing to do yet who never stop complaining is drowning the efforts of those who immerse themselves in their work and endure humiliation for the sake of their mission. Sometimes adopting a lofty tone and sometimes in a lower key, people are attacking and re-placing those tasks which go on one after the other, day after day, year after year, firmly and indomitably.

"It's really immoral to put us on a train like this!"

"Try to make the best of it. In the past there weren't any railways!"

"Army transport always uses sealed boxcars, if they didn't people would know."

"Too bad if someone has the runs, there aren't any lavatories in these carriages."

"But no one would pee in his trousers."

"What can you do? Every Spring Festival more than a billion people want to take the train. . . ."

Listening to these exchanges in the darkness, Yue Zhifeng grew calmer. True, there hadn't been a railway here, or a highway or even a bicycle track. Rich people went by donkey, poor people on their own two feet. Peasants loaded with 1,500 eggs would set out before dawn, and arrive at X city at dusk after passing over innumerable hills and valleys. My beloved, beautiful and yet impoverished land! You should also get richer. Memories of the past are thinning already like smoke or mist but can never be completely forgotten. History, history; reality, reality; ideals, ideals; *mou — mou — mou* — screech — screech — clang — clang. . . . The highway along the Rhine River. Grapes on the hillsides. The dark green river current. Spinning at full speed.

Isn't that children in Frankfurt? Boys and girls with brown hair and blue eyes, chasing, running, jumping, cheering. Feeding the little birds, carrying armfuls of flowers, blowing brass bugles, holding up flags. Sounds of happy life. Friendly, moving cries. Red, pink and white roses. Purple violets and blue forget-me-nots.

No, it isn't Frankfurt. It's his home district on the
northwest plateau. A huge white lilac blossoms over
the grey tiles on the roof. Like snow, like white jade,
like flying foam. Picking a bright green willow leaf,
rolling it into a small tube, looking up at the sky and
clouds, blowing a shrill whistle. Startling two little
orioles into flight. Carrying a small basket over his
arm, going to pick vegetables with his sister. Throwing
stones, chasing wild rabbits, gathering mottled blue
quail eggs. Every little puppy, kitten, calf and foal are
playing. Even each blade of grass is dancing.

No, it isn't the northwest plateau. It's pre-Liberation
Beijing. The school committee under the city works department (headed by Comrade Liu Ren) of the Party's
North China Bureau organized a big gathering of students from Beiping and Tianjin. A camp-fire party.
"The sun goes down behind the mountains and will rise
up as always tomorrow. . . . My youth like a little bird
will not return." "Who tills the barren mountain land,
who plants the flowers on the ground?" One song after
another stirred their young hearts. Finally from every
throat poured the defiant sound that struck terror into
the Kuomintang Special Service, "Unity is strength . . .
death to all undemocratic regimes!" Faith and happiness
can never be parted.

No, it isn't Beijing now past and gone. It's the liberated capital, where the five-starred red flag flut-
ters. It's the first love of his youth, the first warm
breeze to open the doors of his heart. Spring Festival
had just passed, when suddenly he noticed that the
wind was no longer so cold and harsh. The February
wind brought warm hopes, news of early spring. He
ran to Beihai, where the ice had not yet thawed. Still

no tourists around. He took off his cap and undid the top button of his coat. Was it still winter? Of course it was still winter. But it was the winter that leads into spring, the bridge between winter and spring. The wind was proof, the wind was not cold any more! The wind get milder and milder. As if you were getting drunk, fascinated. He welcomed, revelled in the "spring" wind, which felt bitterly cold to others but which made him leap for joy, and softly called the name of the girl he secretly loved.

Is it . . . is it . . . what is it then? Is it a goldfish, a river snail? Is it a water-chestnut, a strawberry? Is it a reed fowl hatching her eggs? Is it a mountain spring, an elm pod, wheat seedlings that have turned green, mating swallows? He drew himself together. It is spring, it is life, it is the time of youth. Doesn't everything — our life, the hearts of each of us, Orion and Cassiopeia, every atomic nucleus, every proton, neutron and meson — contain the vitality, the voices of spring?

He drew himself together and rubbed his eyes. He was clearly aware of the children in Frankfurt singing, of course, it was in German. Alongside the joyful children's chorus, there was a persistent husky woman's voice accompanying it.

He drew himself together again, rubbed his eyes again and became clearly aware that he was in the sealed boxcar from X city to N district. Through the darkness and the din, he heard a children's chorus singing in German, and a husky, inexperienced and rather strained woman's voice accompanying it.

What? A tape-recorder. To hear a tape-recorder in this place! After one song came another, and at the end was an adult's song. After the three songs came the click of the rewind button, and then the three songs began afresh. The persistent, husky and inexperienced woman's voice also started again. The sound of it covered the rest of the din.

The train's long whistle. The shifting square patch of light on the opposite wall reduced its speed and became brighter. In the dusk the passengers who had been individual shadows gradually appeared as substantial forms and outlines. The train was brightly illuminated once, twice — they were probably going through a junction. Then they arrived at a station. Scree — ch, the iron door opened and the glare of the lamps on the station platform lit up the carriage. Yue Zhifeng could see that the tape-recorder was sitting on the knee of the woman with the child. People began to get on and off. On its owner's command, the tape-recorder stopped its song with a click.

"The tape-recorder . . . what brand is it?" asked Yue Zhifeng.

"Sanyo. The people here call it 'Small Goat' for a joke," the woman lifted her head and gave a direct, open answer. It seemed to Yue Zhifeng that her face had known wind and frost but was still youthful and pretty.

"Did you get it in Beijing?" Yue Zhifeng asked again, not knowing why he was so interested. Actually he was not at all a garrulous man.

"No, here." It was not clear whether she referred to X city or some smaller county town where the train was heading. He stared at the Sanyo trademark.

"Are you studying foreign songs?" Yue Zhifeng asked again.

The woman laughed with some embarrassment. "No, I am studying a foreign language." Her smiling face was both modest and noble.

"German?"

"Oh, yes. I haven't got very far."

"What songs are they?" A young man sitting at Yue Zhifeng's feet asked. Yue Zhifeng's continued questions had aroused more people.

"They are *A Little Bird Comes Back to Me, May Polka* and *The First Tobacco Flower*," the woman comrade said. "*Himmel* — heaven, *Vogel* — bird, *Blume* — flower," she said in a low voice to herself.

Their talk did not continue further. The carriage was filled as before with shouts like "Don't push!" "You can't sit on that box!" "Don't tread on the child!" and "There's no room over here!"

"Attention, everyone!" a man wearing a people's police uniform boarded the train, holding a battery-operated megaphone in his hand, and made an announcement with pauses to catch his breath. "Two crooks just now got on the carriage ahead, these hooligans take advantage of the crowd to pick pockets. There is a small number of scoundrels who specialize in robbing people in sealed boxcars. We have arrested these two crooks. Every passenger should increase his vigilance, cooperate closely and carry out a resolute struggle against criminal offenders. Is that clear to everyone?"

"Yes!" chorused the passengers like schoolchildren.

Bustling in satisfaction the railway policeman jumped down from the train, megaphone in hand, and was probably off to another carriage to spread his message.

Yue Zhifeng instinctively felt round for his own two

pieces of luggage and in his four jacket pockets and three trouser pockets. All were still there safe and sound.

The train started. After some short-term confusion while everyone found a place, everyone took up his own position. The conversationalists chatted, the sleepers dozed, the nibblers cracked melon seeds, and the smokers puffed away. The "Small Goat" started up again, with *A Little Bird Comes Back to Me, May Polka* and *The First Tobacco Flower*. She was still studying German, still singing in a low voice, *Himmel* — heaven, *Vogel* — bird, *Blume* — flower.

Who was she? Was she young? Was it her child she was holding? Where did she work? Was she doing scientific or technical work? Was she one of the new students at evening college? Why was she studying German so earnestly? Was she catching up for lost time? Wouldn't she rest for a single minute? Did she have opportunities to meet German friends or to go to Germany or had she already been to Germany? Was she from Beijing or from this area? Did she often come by train? There were many questions he wanted to ask.

"Let's listen to some music," she said. It seemed as if she was speaking to him. Yes, after the third song, she didn't push the rewind button. After *The First Tobacco Flower* came a waltz by Johann Strauss, *Voices of Spring*. The sealed boxcar was swaying gently in time with the spring melody, lifted on waves of pleasure, drifting forward.

They reached Yue Zhifeng's home village. A small station, a one-minute stop. The bell rang for the train's arrival and then immediately rang again for its departure. Yue Zhifeng got off the train with his two pieces of luggage. There was no platform at this small stop and no steps on the boxcar. Each carriage had an ordinary wooden ladder which was brought out when needed. After Yue Zhifeng got down from these crude steps he let out a long sigh. He said goodbye to the woman comrade. The woman responded. He felt some reluctance to go. He had barely got off the train and was still waiting to hand over his ticket and leave when the train moved off. He looked at the rusty, shabby exterior of the sealed boxcar: the paint had worn off in places, leaving patches which seemed white or mottled in the lamplight. However, something he only noticed after he got off the train was that the locomotive was a beauty, with a brand-new, immaculately clean, light-weight diesel engine. Diesel engines were far superior to their predecessors, there were no diesels in Watt's time. The diesel locomotive was pulling forward a long line of sealed boxcars. A moon rose in the sky. Around the station was a thin layer of snow. The sky and snow were both suffused by a bluish light. One could see the black dwarfed pine trees in the distant graveyard. He turned his head, hoping for another look at the sealed boxcar brought into temporary service, packed with birds, May, tobacco flowers and Strauss's magical voices of spring. It seemed that never before had he heard such moving songs. He felt that there was now a new turn for the better in every corner of life, that everything was full of interest, hope and un-forgettable impressions. The melody of spring, the code of life, these things were extremely precious.

Translated by Bonnie S. McDougall

Kite Streamers

BESIDE the white-on-red slogan "Long Live the Great People's Republic of China!", its exclamation mark squeezed tightly against it, towered a two-storey high advertisement for Triangle brand spoons, forks and knives. Together with its neighbours — advertising Xinghai brand pianos, Great Wall travelling cases, Snow Lily cashmere sweaters, Goldfish pencils — it received the meek kisses bestowed by the loyal lights and revealed a glossy, covetous smile. Lean and unyielding willows and two friendly cypresses, one large, the other small, used their random, elegant shadows to console a lawn robbed of its freshness by the west wind. Between the loud billboards and the solitary lawn Fan Susu stood in a relentless early winter night wind. She wore a trim apricot coat, well-ironed grey polyester pants and pert, low-heeled black leather shoes. Around her neck her snow-white gauze scarf resembled the down of a swallow and complimented eyes and hair which were blacker than the night.

"Let's meet by those upstarts," she had said to Jiayuan on the phone. She always referred to this row of billboards as "upstarts", endearing as well as enviable new idols which had all of a sudden sprung into being.

"The more you look, the more you think you too could have a piano," Jiayuan had said.

"Sure, and if you keep on saying, 'kill or be killed', often enough, you become an animal yourself," she answered.

Twenty minutes had gone by, but Jiayuan had still not turned up. He was always late. Fool, have you been blackmailed again? Early one winter morning he had been cycling to the library. On his way he had seen an old woman groaning by the side of the road. Whoever had knocked her down had run away long before she knew what had happened. He had gone over and helped her up, asked her where she lived, locked his bicycle, left it by the roadside and taken her home. As a result, the old woman's family and neighbours had all come out and surrounded him, thinking he was the culprit. And that dim-sighted old woman, egged on and bombarded with questions, had insisted that it was Jiayuan who had run her down. Was it the confusion of old age? Was she driven by some negative intuition that regards all strangers as enemies? When he told the whole story, explaining that all he had done was to offer his help, a woman had shouted in a creaking voice, "Are you trying to tell us that you are a 'Lei Feng' sort of person?"* A guffaw burst from the crowd. That had happened in 1975, when everyone had studied Xunzi and believed that human nature was fundamentally bad.**

He was always late, and always so busy he didn't even have time to clean the stains and dirt on his glasses. Before she met him Susu had never been busy. If a button on her coat was loose she didn't bother to fix

---

* Lei Feng was a young soldier who was singled out in the early 1960s as a model for people to emulate.

** Xunzi was a 3rd century BC philosopher known principally for his theory that human nature in its original state is evil.

it, but left it dangling instead. With the exception of her grandmother's warmth, everything about this city was cold and unwelcoming. When the city had thrown her out, she had only been sixteen. To say "thrown out" is not exactly fair. Salvoes of firecrackers had been set off, and brass bugles sounded to summon her to the vast countryside. In addition, there were red flags, red books, red armbands, red hearts and red oceans, a red world to be built. All the nine hundred million people in this world, from eight to eighty, formed a circle and recited quotations from Chairman Mao in unison shouting, "Kill to the left! Kill to the right! Kill! Kill! Kill!" Her longing for this kind of world had been stronger even than her earlier desire for a kite with two bells. However, she never saw this red world, she saw a green one instead: grass, crops. She had acclaimed this green world. Afterwards it became a yellow world: dead leaves, dirt, the bare land of winter. She became homesick. Then came a black world. That was when her eye-sight was affected by a vitamin deficiency after seeing her companions pull strings to leave the countryside.

Her dream of a bright red world had been lost in the changing of green to yellow and then to black. She began to lose her appetite, started having stomach trouble and became emaciated. Aside from the red dream, there had been lots of other dreams of different colours which she had lost or discarded, which had been snatched away in uproar and chaos, or stolen stealthily. The white dream had been about a navy uniform and sea spray; a professor of medicine and a machinist; about Snow White. Why is every snowflake uniformly hexagonal and yet always changing? Doesn't Nature also have the character of an artist? The blue dream was about the sky, the bottom of the sea, starlight, steel, a champion fencer and parachute jumping; about chemistry flasks and spirit lamps. Oh, yes, and there had been an orange dream, a dream of love! Where was he? Tall, handsome, intelligent, kind-hearted, always smiling good-naturedly.... "Here I am!" she once shouted to the Echoing Wall at the Temple of Heaven.

Dad and mum had tried every means possible and asked as many people as they could to help get her back to the city which had bestowed, generously, so many dreams upon her. Her father had finally realized that it was unavoidable. The story of what he had gone through to get her back was another dream, strange and absurd. She no longer cared for that sort of dream, nor did she care for that kind of life or the title "Gallant Shepherd Girl". She seldom, if ever, brought up that name and those differently-coloured sides of her life.

She returned having lost many colours but having gained strength, and added a number of odours: oil, mashed garlic, fried golden spring onion; drinkers' hiccups, steam, sheep's-head meat sliced thinner than paper. She now worked as a waitress in a Muslim canteen, though she was not a Muslim. Presenting flowers, congratulations, straight A grades, extraordinary good news, trains, cars, parades, tears of joy, Red Guards brandishing leather belts against class enemies, recitations of "the highest instructions", green and maroon horses, the look on the production team leader's face. . . . Was all this aimed at a plate containing three ounces of fried dough? One day she found a picture of herself which had been taken when she was seven. It was National Day, 1959. She was wearing plaits with two big butterfly bows which flew with her up to the sky. Along with her teacher she flew up to the rostrum in Tian An Men Square and presented flowers to Chairman Mao. Chairman Mao shook hands with her. She was small and had never shaken hands with anybody before. Chairman Mao's hand was big, thick, warm and strong. Chairman Mao seemed to say something but she didn't catch it. Afterwards she recalled vaguely that it was something like "little child". How lucky she was. She was Chairman Mao's "little child" and she would be happy for ever and ever.

But afterwards she was not sure whether it really was a picture of her. Had it actually happened? She couldn't recognize herself. Neither when she came back to the city in 1975 could she recognize Chairman Mao. In the past Chairman Mao used to stand straight and his movements were energetic. But now when she saw him on the newsreel's "News in Brief", it seemed that he had difficulty moving his feet, that he opened his mouth and was unable to shut it again for a long time. But all day the newspapers and radio kept publicizing noisily his ambiguous "latest instructions". She felt sad and wanted to go and see Chairman Mao and prepare a bowl of yam soup for him. When grandma fell ill, she had made her soup with white, velvety, finely cut chunks of yam, sweet hot, and tasty. It was a tonic for a weak old person. No, she didn't want to tell Chairman Mao about her anxieties and grievances, mustn't bother him. If she started crying in his presence, she would have to turn her face away.

But this was all impossible. Was she no longer fortunate? Had her luck run out at the age of seven? What

had she come back to the city for? For mother? Ridiculous! For grandmother! No, that wasn't why. The papers said that everything you did was for Chairman
Mao, but she couldn't see him! So Susu stopped dreaming.   Nevertheless, she kept talking, tossing, sighing,
grinding her teeth in her sleep. "Susu wake up!"
said her mother. She woke up, lost, unable to remember
her dream and felt only a cold sweat on her forehead
and an ache all over, as though she had just been carried out of a contagious diseases ward.

She happened to be at the roadside the day the fool-
ish Jiayuan was falsely accused for his kindness to the
old woman, saw him surrounded and attacked. Jiayuan
was not tall or good-looking, and always wore a naive
smile which she seemed to have known long ago.

Afterwards a policeman came to the scene. This policeman was as clever as King Solomon. "Get two wit-
nesses to testify that you didn't knock down the old
woman," he said. "Otherwise you did." "Can you get
two people to testify that you're not a KGB agent? If
not, then you will be executed," Susu thought to herself
although she didn't, in fact, utter a sound. All she was
doing was watching an interesting scene before going to
work.   There was row upon row of watchers because
it was free and more novel than the theatre and cin-
ema, where all you heard was "soaring to the heavens",
"soaring to the empyrean" or "conquer the heavens",
"shooting through the clouds and sky".* They could
write of nothing but annoying the "sky".

"What do you want? Should I be punished just because I did her a good turn?" The naive smile became

---

* Expressions popular during the "cultural revolution".

wide, agonized eyes. Susu felt a thorn pricking at her heart and wanted to vomit. She stumbled away, hoping that King Solomon was not chasing after her.

It so happened that that evening the young fool came to the canteen to have fried dough chips. He was all smiles again. He only ordered two ounces.

"Is two ounces enough for you?" Susu intuitively changed her practice of not chatting with customers.

"Well, I'll have two ounces to start with," said the young fool apologetically. He crooked the second finger of his right hand to push up his glasses which, in fact, did not seem to be slipping down his nose.

"If you haven't got enough money or grain coupons," she said without realizing why, "it doesn't matter. Eat now and pay for the rest tomorrow."

"What about the canteen regulations?"

"I'll pay for you. It's nothing to do with the regulations."

"Thank you. In that case I'll have some more. I didn't have enough to eat for lunch."

"Do you want a *jin* and a half?"

"Oh, no, six ounces will do."

"Okay." She got him four ounces more. When the chef found out Susu knew the customer, he ladled out an extra portion of diced mutton. Each piece of dough had been freshly fried and they glittered on the plate like gold beans. The light from the gold beans shone on the young man's face and his smile became even more attractive. For the first time Susu understood that fried dough chips were a great and powerful treasure.

"They said that I knocked her down while cycling and took away all my money and grain coupons."

"But you didn't, did you?"

"Of course not."

"Why did you give them the money? You shouldn't have given them a penny! What an insult!"

"Look, that old woman needed money and grain coupons badly. Besides, I didn't want to waste my time getting angry." Customers across the room were calling. "Coming!" she shouted, and left, cloth in hand.

After she got home that night, she thought of telling her grandmother about that fool. But grandma had had an angina attack. Her father and mother couldn't decide whether or not they should send her to hospital immediately. "The emergency room of that hospital is stinking, unbearable. If anyone survives after lying there for five hours, it proves that their internal organs are made of iron," said Susu. Her father glared at her reproachfully for being so heartless about grandma. She turned and left for her room, a makeshift extra room.

That night Susu had a dream. It was a dream she'd often had years ago — about flying a kite. But each time it had been different. She hadn't had that kind of dream since 1966, and she had not had any dreams at all for the six years since 1970. Water filled the long-dried river bed. The long-blocked roads reopened to traffic, the dreams reappeared. But this time it was not from the lawn or the playground, but from horseback that the kite was being flown. And it wasn't Susu flying it but the young man who had eaten six ounces of fried dough chips. The kite was simply made, shabby enough to make you cry! Long and rectangular, it was known locally as a "botty curtain". It flew up, higher even than the new wing of the Dongfeng Hotel, the pine trees on the hill and the eagles over the grassland. It flew higher too than the balloon saying "Long Live the Great Proletarian Cultural Revolution!" It flew and flew over mountains, rivers, rows of pines, groups of Red Guards, herds of horses and plates of fried dough chips. How wonderful! She too began to fly along after that "botty curtain", and became a long streamer trailing behind it.

She awoke from the dream. Dawn had not yet broken. She shone a torch looking for the photograph of that happiest of times. At the tenth anniversary of the founding of the People's Republic of China she had presented flowers to Chairman Mao. She thought herself a fortunate person. Humming the song "All Commune Members Are Sunflowers", she repaired the button which she had left loose and dangling for so long. Then she spontaneously wished Chairman Mao good health. She made some yam soup for her grandmother. The soup would have an almost magical effect. Her grandmother would feel better as soon as she drank it. By now it was getting brighter. Her family and neighbours were all up. She began to brush her teeth and wash with great delight, all the while making noises as if a train were rumbling through their courtyard. Her washing sounded like the legendary Nezha storming the ocean. She ate some leftover steamed bread together with hot pickled vegetables. Only when she drank a bowl of boiled water did she feel she was re-entering the real world from the "botty curtain" and in the moment doubted whether the article "Boiled Water is the Best Drink" had really been attacking the "three red banners".* She tied her

---

* An article in the *Beijing Evening News* which was criticized for attacking the "three red banners", namely, "the General Line, the Great Leap Forward and People's Commune".

shoelaces and walked with a thumping sound as though iron nails had been driven into her heels or a peg was being hammered into a board to make a Czecho-slovakian-style cabinet.

"What are you so happy about, Susu?" asked her father.

"I'm going to be promoted to director," Susu answered.

Her father was overjoyed. When, at the age of six, she had been selected as group leader in the kindergarten, her father had been so happy he kept telling everybody he met about it. When at nine, she was serving as a captain in the Young Pioneers he was in heaven. . . . When the steam whistle of the train tooted, he had suddenly burst into tears, his face convulsed, ghastly. All the children except Susu had cried too. Susu took it much more in her stride than her father. She seemed determined to find an outlet for her talent and resolved to become a great success.

"Hello! You're back. What would you like today?"

"First, let me settle my account. Here's four ounces worth of grain coupons and the money, twenty-eight *fen*."

"You take it so seriously."

"I guess I'll have four ounces of fried dough chips again."

"Why don't you have something else for a change? We've got ravioli, seven to the ounce for fifteen *fen*; dumplings, two per ounce, eighteen *fen*; beancurd jelly with sesame cakes, only thirty *fen* for four ounces."

"I'll have whatever's quickest."

"Just a second. There's another customer. ; . . I'll

get you some dumplings then. Do you want six ounces again? . . . Here they are. Why are you so busy? Are you a student?"

"Do you think I'm capable of being that?"

"Then maybe you're a technician, an accordionist, or a new guy promoted to a top job."

"Is that what I look like?"

"Well, what do you do. . . ?"

"I don't have a job."

"Hold on a minute, here comes another customer. . . . If you don't have a job why are you so busy?"

"A jobless person is also a human being with a life to lead, youth, lots of things to do."

"What keeps you so busy then?"

"Reading."

"Reading? Reading what?"

"Optimization, palaeontology, foreign languages."

"Are you going to take a university entrance exam?"

"Do universities admit students by entrance exam nowadays? Anyway, I'm not the kind of person who would turn in a blank exam paper."

"It's a pity Zhang Tiesheng's* way of getting into college doesn't work."

"We're still young. We should learn something useful, don't you think?" He finished his dumplings and hurried off, leaving the puzzle unsolved.

He was punctual, and came at the same time as before. This time he ordered beancurd jelly, the grey bean curd jelly with green chive flowers and mud-like

---

* Zhang Tiesheng was a student who turned in a blank paper in a university extrance exam and was later admitted to college. He was held up by the "gang of four" as a hero who rebelled against the "old educational system".

sesame jam with red pepper spread on top of it. Why is it that people in China and abroad know the name of the first emperor of the Qin Dynasty but not the name of the scientific genius who invented beancurd jelly?

"You lied to me."

"No, I didn't."

"You told me you didn't have a job."

"It's true. I came back from the north only three months ago. The reason I gave for leaving was 'personal business'. But I start a job next month."

"In a scientific research institute?"

"No, in a neighbourhood service centre. I'll be apprenticed to learn how to repair umbrellas."

"That's terrible!"

"No, it's not. If you've got a broken umbrella, bring it to me."

"What about your optimization methods, palaeontology and foreign languages?"

"I'll go on studying."

"Are you going to repair umbrellas by the optimization method, or make an umbrella out of dinosaur bones?"

"Well, optimization could also be applied to umbrella repairing. The thing is, however. . . . I'd like another bowl of beancurd jelly, not too much pepper, please . . . you can see the perspiration on my forehead . . . thank you. You know, you take a job to make a living and also to do your duty. But a person should be more than just his trade. A job isn't everything, nor does it last for ever. Human beings should be the masters of the world and their work, and above all, masters of knowledge. Suppose both of us are

umbrella repairers, and we each earn eighteen yuan a
month. But then if you know about dinosaurs whereas
I don't, you're better off and richer than I am. Am I
right?"

"I don't know what you're talking about."

"Yes you do. In fact, you already did. Otherwise,
why would you be talking to me? Look, that customer
from Shandong over there is getting angry because he
got some grit in his boiled peanuts and he's hurt his
teeth. Goodbye!"

"Bye! See you tomorrow."

On uttering the word "tomorrow", Susu flushed.
Tomorrow was, like the streamers tied to that "botty
curtain", simple and unadorned, easy and unrestrained.
It was like bamboos, clouds, dreams, ballet, a note from
a G string, like autumn leaves and spring flowers. But
it was a "botty curtain" only a poor, bare-bottomed
child could afford to fly.

He didn't come the following day. Nor did he
come the day after that. And looking for that foal,
Susu lost her own way and moaned like a sad whinny-
ing mare. It was as if her residence registration, grain
certificates and ration cards had been revoked in one
fell swoop.

"It's you! You're . . . back again!"

"My grandmother died."

Leaning against the wall, Susu felt as if she had
fallen into an ice pit. It was some time before she
realized that this bespectacled young fool's grandmother was not her own grandmother. Yet she still
felt saddened and cold all over.

"One's life is short, and time is the most precious
thing."

"But my most precious time is spent carrying plates."
She smiled heavily and seemed to hear the distant
sound of a galloping colt.

"You've carried plates for a lot of people. We
should thank you. But it's more than that."

"What else? They don't really even need me to
carry dishes. It wasn't easy for my dad and mum to
get this job for me. They had to go to a lot of trouble."

"It's the same everywhere," he said with an understanding smile. "I suggest you learn some Arabic since
this is a Muslim canteen."

"What's so special about a Muslim canteen? Any-
how, the Egyptian ambassador won't be coming here
for fried dough chips."

"But you might be the ambassador to Egypt. Have
you ever thought of that?"

"You're joking," she said. The colt raced into the
Muslim canteen and trod on her feet. "That's just
dreaming."

"Dreaming, joking, what's wrong with that? Otherwise life would be too dull, wouldn't it? Besides, you
should be confident that you could develop the talents,
the qualifications and abilities to be an ambassador to
Egypt, or, better still, overtake him. You may not
serve as an ambassador, but you should be able to
surpass him. The key to achievement is study."

"You sound like a rather ambitious careerist."

"No. Like Adam."

"What is Adam?"

"It's the first Arabic word I am going to teach you.
Adam means person. It's a beautiful word. Adam in
the Garden of Eden. It is a transliteration. And Eve
is pronounced *Hawa,* meaning sky. Human beings

need the sky and the sky in turn needs human beings."

"So that's why from childhood onwards we fly kites?"

"See, you're an exceptional student."

Lesson one: Human beings. Adam needs Eve and Eve needs Adam. Human beings need the sky and the sky needs human beings. We need kites, balloons, airplanes, rockets and spaceships. That was how she started to learn Arabic. It made people roundabout a little uneasy. "You should keep your mind on carrying dishes. Be careful not to make a bad impression. Do you have any friends or relatives abroad? If the purification-of-class-ranks movement starts again, strange people, strange things and strange phenomena will be examined. You'll be placed under investigation as a special case." "I haven't dropped a single plate. I don't wish to be promoted to director. I know Muhammad, Sadat and Arafat. You are entirely welcome to be chief of my special-case examination group."

Besides, she was in love with Jiayuan. The news soon reached her father's ears. It was as though cameras and bugging devices, all shadowing the young girl, were omnipresent. "What's his name, his original name, any other names he's ever used? His family background, his own background? What was their economic situation before and after land reform. His personal history since he was three months old? His political record? Are there any members of his family or immediate relatives who were sentenced to death or imprisonment, put under surveillance, or were landlords, rich peasants, counter-revolutionaries, bad elements, Rightists? When were they labelled as Rightists? And when were the labels removed? How did he act in past political movements? His and his family members' incomes and expenditures, bank deposits and balances. . . ?"

To all of these questions, Susu had no answers. Her mother was so frightened she cried. "You're only twenty-four years and seven months old. You're not supposed to think about marriage for another five months yet. There are bad people around everywhere, you know." Dad was resolved to see the young man's neighbourhood committee, his work unit, local police station, personnel department and file department, anywhere he might be known. To get things moving, he planned to give a hot-pot dinner for the relevant people and accordingly started to make preparations. His favourite Yixing teapot was flung to the ground and smashed into pieces.

"The way you are doing things, you might find counter-revolutionaries but you would never find a friend!" Susu shouted and then burst into tears.

The director, members of the management, group leader and instructor all raised questions like her father's and gave advice like her mother's. A proletarian love should grow out of a shared belief, a shared point of view and a shared ideology, and a mutual and deep understanding should be cultivated seriously, cautiously and sincerely over a long period. One must always be on the alert for enemy activities. The choice of one's love should follow the five conditions for a young revolutionary. She couldn't throw the restaurant's teapot on the floor since she had been trained since childhood to protect public property.

Chairman Mao passed away. Susu shook and cried bitterly. She had wanted to cry long ago, to cry for Chairman Mao, to cry for herself and for others.

"China is finished!" said her father, but instead it was the end of the "gang of four". Susu was close to Chairman Mao a second time when she paid respects to his remains. "I once came to present flowers to you," she said quietly and calmly.

She knew that everything was changing. She could openly and casually learn Arabic although the fact remained that admission to the Party and promotion came easier for those who spent the whole night playing poker than for those who studied foreign languages. She could walk hand-in-hand with Jiayuan, although some people went crazy at the sight of young men and women together. But they still couldn't find a place to talk. The chairs in the park were always occupied. After trying hard they eventually did find one but it turned out that there was a pool of vomit in front of it. They moved on to a large, ramshackle park where loudspeakers hung from the telegraph poles beside every bench. The loudspeakers were blaring out "Information for Visitors", ". . . fifty *fen* to fifteen yuan fine", ". . . will be sent to the relevant law-enforcing authority", "conscientiously observe the regulations and obey the administrative personnel", etc. The regulations were so complicated a person wouldn't even know how to stroll in the park without first taking a week's training course. How could they possibly sit there and talk about their love? They left.

But where to? By the side of the moat was a place

without loudspeakers, but it was somewhat out-of-the-way. Once, it was said, a courting young couple had been whispering there. All of a sudden, they heard "Don't move!" and a masked man appeared, dagger in hand. Next to him stood an accomplice. Their watches were stolen and the money taken from their pockets. Lovers are always powerless in the face of violence. The case was cracked by the police and the perpetrators arrested. Why do some people dislike the police department? No one could do without them.

What about going to a restaurant? Well, first you have to position yourself behind someone's chair and watch him eat, mouthful by mouthful, then light a cigarette and stretch himself. Not long after you take this hard-to-come-by seat and pick up your chopsticks, your newly-arrived successor places his foot on the rung of your chair. As he moves his leg, the diced meat and slices of tripe you're eating begin to dance in your throat. Should you want to go to a bar or a coffee shop, you won't be able to find one because those are decadent places. Taking a walk will keep you in trim and is a fashion in America. But in winter it's too cold. Of course they did go out together in that cold weather, twenty degrees below zero, wearing padded coats, fur hats, woollen scarves and face masks. Hygienic and infection-free. But what often happens to courting couples is that naughty children playing in the lanes burst out laughing, or curse and throw stones at them. It makes you wonder how these brats ever came into this world.

Jiayuan was easy-going about things. He didn't mind where they went. Whether it was leaning against a railing, or sitting beneath a parasol tree or on the riverbank, he just wanted to stop and sit awhile, speak in Arabic and English and snuggle up to Susu. But Susu was always dissatisfied, difficult to please. No, she didn't want to accept that kind of substitute, in the same way that the customer from Shandong couldn't tolerate the grit in his peanuts. For three years now they had spent their weekends looking for somewhere to sit down. They kept on looking and whole evenings disappeared. Oh, my boundless sky and vast land, on which tiny piece of you may young people court, embrace and kiss? All we need is a small, small place. You can hold great heroes, earth-shaking rebels, vicious destroyers and dissolute scoundrels. You can hold battlefields, demolition sites, city squares, meeting halls, execution grounds . . . why can't you find a place for Susu, 1.6 metres tall and 48 kilos in weight, and for Jiayuan, just under 1.7 metres and 54 kilos, who are head over heels in love?

Susu rubbed her burning eyes. Had she touched some pepper? Had she rubbed her eyes because they were burning or were her eyes burning because she'd rubbed them? "Can we find a place to stay this evening?" she wondered. Though the weather was getting colder, it wasn't yet necessary to wear a face mask. Jiayuan said that he would go to see the Housing Administration Department. They would get married as soon as they found a place. They wouldn't have to walk in the lanes any longer.

"Hey, Comrade Elder Sister, can you tell me where Dashi Street is?" asked a man with an accent, a big bundle on his back and dust all over his new clothes. He was actually much older than Susu.

"Dashi Street?   This is Dashi Street," answered Susu, pointing to the intersection where the traffic lights were changing, and the cars, buses and bicycles were surging ahead, stopping and then rushing forward again like the tide.

"Is this really Dashi Street?"   His back bent, the middle-aged man looked up and rolled his eyes, expressing doubt.

"It *is* Dashi Street," Susu repeated emphatically. She wished she could show this honest, skeptical person the department store and the big roast duck restaurant by holding them all in the palm of her hand.   The man hesitantly took a few steps.   He went to cross the street, but not at the pedestrian crossing.   A white-uniformed traffic policemen shouted at him through a loudspeaker.   Alarmed and confused by the tongue-lashing, the man halted in the middle of the road, surrounded by a whirlpool of automobiles.   "Comrade Elder Brother," the man asked, tilting back his head, "where is Dashi Street?"

"Susu!" Jiayuan arrived, breathless, his hair dishevelled, his forehead dripping with sweat.

"Did you just burrow up out of the ground?   I've been waiting ages for you.   You don't show up and then all of a sudden you appear out of nowhere."

"I know how to make myself invisible.   In fact, I've been following you."

"If only we both knew that trick. . . ."

"What do you mean?"

"Then nobody could see us if we danced in the park."

"Why are you talking so loudly?   People are looking at you."

"Some people think dancing is vulgar because they're so ugly themselves."

"You're sounding more and more sarcastic. You weren't like this before."

"It must be the autumn wind sharpening up my tongue. We can't even find a place to shelter from it."

Jiayuan's eyes were dim and Susu lowered her head. Multitudes of lights, windows and houses were reflected in the lens of his glasses.

"No flat?"

"No. The Housing Administration Department refused to let us have one. They told me there are people who've been married for several years and have kids that still don't have a place."

"Well, where did they get married then? In a park? In the kitchen where the dough chips are made? In the traffic policemen's kiosk? That would be a good place with glass on all sides. Or maybe in a cage at the zoo? But that would send up the price of tickets."

"Don't get so touchy. What you. . . ." He pushed back the glasses which were unlikely to slip off. "What you said is no doubt correct. But you can't expect houses to drop out of the sky. There are so many people who need houses. And some of them really are in a more difficult position than we are."

Susu was reduced to silence. Lowering her head, she began to kick a non-existent pebble.

"Well, have you had supper? I haven't." Jiayuan changed the subject.

"What did you say? Oh, I only remember serving meals, never whether I've eaten myself."

"I take it you haven't then. Let's go to that *wonton* canteen. You stand in the queue and I'll try to get a seat. Or I'll get a seat while you line up."

"You're repeating yourself. You sound like somebody making a speech at a meeting."

The *wonton* canteen was crowded. You would have thought the *wonton* was free, or better yet that you'd be paid to eat it instead of paying twenty *fen* per bowl. "Let's forget about the *wonton* and buy some sesame cakes instead. Oh, there's a queue for that too. Then let's go and get some buns from the store across the street." But just as they got there and reached out for the buns, the salesclerk was selling the last two to a little old man wearing a Qing-dynasty robe lined with badger fur. "Well, let's forget about the buns. But what can we do?"

"It would have been great if we just hadn't been born in the first place," Susu said coldly. "If Ma Yinchu's* new population theory hadn't been mistakenly criticized we would never have come into this world."

"Why are you in such a bad temper? Anyway, we actually came into the world before his population theory existed. Since the fruit buns are sold out, let's buy a couple of bags of biscuits. We have biscuits. We wait on customers and repair umbrellas. We study, we do good things and help people. And there can never be too many good people — on the contrary, there aren't enough."

---

* Ma Yinchu, ex-president of Beijing University, was criticized during the "cultural revolution" for his theories of family planning and population control, and was rehabilitated after the fall of the "gang of four".

"What's the reward for being a do-doer? To have to hand over seven yuan and two *jin's* worth of grain coupons to somebody who's having you on?"

"In any case, I still should've helped the old woman, even if they had extorted seven hundred yuan.... I suppose you would've done the same thing, wouldn't you? Susu!" Jiayuan suddenly shouted. Thunder and lightning. The electricity wires and lights were swaying.

"Try one of my biscuits," said Jiayuan.

"They're the same as mine."

"No, mine are particularly good."

"Why?"

"Why not? Even two drops of water aren't exactly the same."

"Try mine then."

"Alright, I'll try yours."

"You try mine after I've tried yours."

They exchanged biscuits and then shared them one by one. When they had eaten them all Susu laughed. Hungry people are worse-tempered than the well-fed.

There was a drastic change in the weather. Electricity wires were whining. Billboards were roaring. The street lights became hazy. A rustling cold wind dispersed the pedestrians. In a matter of seconds, the street was broad and empty. Traffic policemen retreated into the kiosks Susu had reckoned were an ideal bridal chamber.

"We must find some shelter!" Icy sleet, falling at an angle, offered a stern caress. They held hands, unable to hear each other speak. Against nature and against life they were undefended. But the big hand

and the smaller hand were both warm. Their own inextinguishable fire was all the property and power they had.

"Let's find somewhere to shelter," they mumbled, chewing dust and rain. They started to run. Whether Jiayuan was pulling Susu, Susu was pulling Jiayuan, or the wind was pushing the two of them was hard to tell. In any case, a burst of energy pulled and shoved them forward. They made their way to a recently-finished fourteen-storey block. They had longed for a place in this newly-born row of high-rises. But they were strangers. An aversion to strangers was one of the characteristics of the old woman who'd been run down and the old man in the badger fur robe. What a look the old boy had given the two of them when they went to buy buns! As though he thought that any minute they would take out daggers.

There had been widespread criticism of this row of high-rises. A family living on a top floor had been unable to carry a wardrobe up to their flat. They then tried to hoist it up through the window. What a marvellous spectacle. The rope broke and the wardrobe fell and was smashed to pieces. A new *Arabian Nights* story. But Susu and Jiayuan thought otherwise. They always felt a little shy approaching the buildings, their longing being a kind of unrequited love.

The snow and rain gave them the courage to dash in. They climbed up storey after storey. The staircase was filthy. There were no lights. There were sockets but no bulbs. Fortunately the street lights were on all night and that was enough. After making numerous turns they eventually reached the corridor on the top floor. It seemed uninhabited. There was a smell of cement and fresh paint and it was warm. No wind, rain or snow. It was devoid of loudspeakers broadcasting instructions, people in masks, pedestrians and impatient customers jiggling your chair to make you leave. Here there were no parents who looked down on umbrella repairers and waitresses. No mischievous children who would, seeing a courting couple, use foul language, abuse and throw stones at them. From here, the lights of the twenty-five storey Dongfeng Hotel were visible. The melodious chiming of the railroad station clock was audible and the electric clock on the customs building could be seen. Looking down, they saw green, orange and silver lights. Electric sparks flashed from the trolley wires. Headlights and red signal lights blinked on and off. They heaved a deep sigh of relief, as though they had reached paradise.

"Are you tired?"

"No, not at all."

"We've climbed fourteen stories."

"I could climb another fourteen."

"So could I."

"That man was a real idiot."

"Who?"

"That country bumpkin we met a while ago. He was at the bottom of Dashi Street but he was still wandering all over the place looking for it. I told him but he wouldn't believe me."

They began to speak in Arabic. Stammering, like their heartbeats, enthusiastic, unconventional. Jiayuan was going to take an entrance exam for graduate school. "We may not succeed," he urged the less-than-confident Susu, "but we should try our best." Jiayuan took her hand in his. It was tender and firm. Susu moved closer and nestled against his ordinary, strong shoulder. Her hair was like warm black rain. The lights — glimmering, flickering and twisting — formed the lines of a poem. An old German ballad goes: "There is a flower called 'forget-me-not', it's blossoms are blue." A Northern Shanxi ballad goes: "Words of love I have for you. Fearing the laughter of others, I hesitate to let you know." Blue flowers floated in the air. Waves washed over them. Why fear being laughed at? Youth is more fiery even than fire itself. It is a pigeon's whistle, fresh flowers, Susu and Jia-yuan's tear-filled eyes.

Clatter . . . clack. . . .

"Who's there?" barked a loud voice. Jiayuan and Susu suddenly became aware of several people at either end of the corridor. Many of them were carrying things: rolling pins, spatulas, shovels. Man is a tool-using animal. You might have thought this was an uprising of primitive citizens.

A harsh and hostile interrogation began: "Who are you? What are you up to? Who are you looking for? Did you say you weren't looking for anyone? That you came here to take shelter from the wind and rain? Damn you! Sneaking around and hugging like that. I bet you were up to no good. Young people nowadays are just impossible. China will be destroyed by the likes of you. Where do you work? Your names? Your original names, any other names you've ever used? Have you got your resident's cards, employee's I.D. cards or letters of introduction? Why don't you stay home? Why don't you stay with your parents, your leaders or the broad masses? No, you can't leave.

Did you think nobody would see you? Whose doors have you pried open? A public place? This public place is ours, not yours. Shame on you! Hooligans! Disgraceful! What? An insult? What do you mean insult? Don't you know we were given half-shaved heads? We were beaten. We were made to do the 'jet-plane'.* Get out of here or we'll show you what we can do. Get the ropes ready. . . ."

Susu and Jiayuan both kept calm. A moment earlier they had been happy. The two of them knew, though not well, several languages. But neither of them could understand this strange language spoken by their dear compatriots. If dinosaurs could talk, they would be more intelligible than this. Confused, they looked at each other and smiled.

"We're going to do something about this," a "dinosaur" plucked up enough courage to say. No sooner had he finished than he went and hid behind the others.

"We're really going to do something about this," others echoed and then shrank back. Jiayuan and Susu were still encircled and blocked, unable to get away.

Suddenly a brave man with a drainpipe in his hand shouted, "Aren't you Susu?"

Susu nodded. With a doubt.

The misunderstanding was cleared up. "Sorry. We apologize. We were afraid of the thief. People say there've been thefts in this building. We have to take precautions. There are some bad types about. We thought you were. . . . How stupid. Sorry."

---

* Punishments inflicted on "bad" elements during the "cultural revolution". In the "jet-plane" the victim was forced to bend down with arms forced upwards for long periods of time.

Susu vaguely recognized the long-haired young man as a classmate from elementary school. He was white-skinned, plump, like a bun made from fine white flour, a food which should be popularized.

"Now that you're at my door. . . ." her schoolmate invited them in. "All right," Susu and Jiayuan winked at each other. They followed her schoolmate to the dazzlingly bright lift. Now they had a legitimate status as the guests of a resident. The door closed and the lift began to drone. Thanks to this kind-hearted schoolmate their security and dignity were assured. The Arabic numerals on the lift wall changed quickly, from 14 to 4, and now the ear-shaped number 3 lit up. It stopped and the door opened. Leaving the lift, they turned one corner after another until they reached his flat. The serrated key, the real trouble-shooter, opened the door confidently with a click. A flicked switch and the lounge and kitchen lights were on. The white walls looked as though they were wearing too much powder. The bedroom door creaked open. A bluish light from the street lamps filled the room. Before Susu could ask her schoolmate not to switch on the light it was on. "Sit down." A twin bed, wardrobe, a red leatherette sofa, a chest of drawers, a tin of malt-and-milk extract, an unopened "ten-delicacy" tonic wine. Her schoolmate continued to introduce his new home: space, amenities, design. Water, heating, gas. Lighting, ventilation, sound-proofing. Fire-proofing, earthquake-proofing.

"You live here all by yourself?"

"Yes," rubbing his hands, the schoolmate was becoming prouder by the minute. "My dad got this place for me. My parents are really anxious for me to get married. I plan to take care of that next May Day. You must come. Good, that's settled. I've got someone to give a hand. He's my friend's uncle and he used to work as a cook at the French embassy. It's going to be both Chinese and foreign food. His best dish is sugar-coated yams. You can wind the sugar threads round and round and they won't break. Don't give me any presents, by the way. Don't buy me furniture or a desk lamp or bedding. I've got everything I need."

"What's your fiancée's name? Where does she work?"

"Oh, that hasn't been decided yet."

"Is she waiting to be assigned a job?"

"No, I mean I haven't made up my mind yet who I'm going to marry. But I'll get somebody before next May Day. No problem."

Susu picked up a balloon from a table and rubbed it vigorously against the leatherette sofa. She tossed it upwards and it clung firmly to the ceiling. Looking up, she delighted in a game she had loved since childhood.

"Oh, good heavens! Why doesn't it come down?" asked the schoolmate, his mouth agape in astonishment. "It's still up there!"

"It's a kind of magic," Susu replied, looking sideways at Jiayuan and pulling a face. They left. Flabbergasted, their hospitable host had yet to regain his composure as he saw them off at the lift. His mind was still on the balloon on the ceiling.

Susu and Jiayuan left their lovely high-rise. It was

still snowing and a wind was still blowing. As it fell on their hands and on their faces and trickled down their necks, the damp snow seemed to express a kind of affection for them.

"It's all my fault," said Jiayuan. "I've got no way of getting that sort of place. I'm sorry I've put you in such a difficult position." Laughing, Susu covered his mouth with her hand. In her happiness, her smiling face would have put a blossoming pomegranate to shame.

Jiayuan understood. He began to laugh too. They both understood their own fortune. They knew that life and the world belonged to them. The laughter of the young couple seemed to halt the wind, snow and rain, and the glow of the night sky over the city was the sun.

Susu ran ahead and Jiayuan chased after her. Beneath the street lamp, the sheets of rain seemed even heavier and more dense.

"This is Dashi Street. It's right here!" shouted Susu at the top of her voice, pointing to the hotel building.

"Of course. I never doubted it."

"We've had a wonderfully happy evening. Now we should shake hands and say goodbye."

"Well, goodbye. We won't meet tomorrow. We must work hard. We both want to pass that entrance exam."

"Well, it's just possible that we will."

"Pleasant dreams!"

"Dreams about what?"

"Dreams about . . . a kite!"

What? A kite? How did he know about that?

"You know about the kite too, do you? Do you know about the streamers hanging from that kite?"

"Why, of course. How could I not?"

Susu ran back to embrace him and kissed him right there in the street. Then they each headed home, turning frequently, as the distance between them grew, to wave to one another.

Translated by Lü Binghong

The Young Newcomer in the Organization Department

IT was March and the sky was heavy with sleet. A pedicab drew to a halt outside the District Party Committee and a young man jumped out. Looking at the sign on the gate the driver said politely: "If you're getting out here, don't worry about the fare." Old Lu, the gateman, a disabled veteran, shuffled out and asked where the young man had come from, while giving him a hand unloading his damp luggage, and then went off to fetch the department secretary, Zhao Huiwen. She emerged and clasped his hands firmly, "We've been waiting for you for a long time." The young man, Lin Zhen by name, had met her before when he had been a primary school teacher. Despite the tired shadows on her pale, attractive face, her eyes still radiated warmth and friendliness. She conducted Lin to the men's dormitory, helped him unpack and hung out his quilt to dry, then made the bed for him. As she did this, she kept smoothing back her hair with her fingers, in the way that pretty and able young women comrades often do.

"We've waited quite a while for you. We wanted to have you transferred here six months ago, but the cultural and educational section of the District People's Committee absolutely refused to let you go. It

was only after the District Party Committee secretary
went to see the District Director and had a set-to with
the Education Bureau people that we were able to get
you transferred."

"But I only heard I was being moved the day before
yesterday. I didn't quite know what to make of it.
What exactly does the work here involve anyway?"

"Just about everything."

"And what about the organization department itself."

"The organization department is in charge of organizational work."

"Is it a busy place?"

"Sometimes."

She cast an eye over his bed, then shook her head
and said with a note of exasperated indulgence:
"Young men never keep anything clean! Just look at
that pillow slip — it's grubby already. The edge of
your quilt cover is filthy with grime from your neck;
and as for this sheet, it's so crumpled it looks like a
piece of seersucker. . . ."

Lin had felt happy as soon as he walked through
the District Party Committee door and, what's more,
he'd now encountered someone who was both warm
and kind.

In a light-hearted mood he went off to Deputy
Director Liu Shiwu's office to report in. Heart pounding, he knocked on the door. He found Liu wreathed
in smoke, pondering over the organization department
work plan. Pushing aside a pile of documents, he
welcomed Lin and motioned him to the sofa while he
sat on a chair next to his desk.

"Everything going alright then?" Liu had a slight nervous tick in his left eye. He tapped his cigarette ash.

"The Party branch secretary told me to come the day after tomorrow, but since I had finished everything I had to do at the school I came today instead. When they told me I was being sent to work in the organization department, I was afraid I wouldn't be up to the job since I've only just joined the Party. Being a primary school teacher is rather different from doing organizational work."

Delivering his prepared speech, Lin felt he sounded as stilted as a child meeting a teacher for the first time. He found the room uncomfortably hot. Although it was mid-March and winter was almost over, the fire was still on. The frost on the window-panes was melting and dirty rivulets trickled down the glass. He wanted to wipe the perspiration from his brow but couldn't find his handkerchief.

Liu mechanically nodded his head and, almost without looking, extracted a cardboard folder from the pile of documents. Opening it, he took out Lin's Party registration form. He frowned with concentration as he skimmed through it with his sharp eyes. He blinked and then stood up, resting his weight on the back of the chair. His padded jacket slipped a little lower on his shoulders. Then he drawled:

"Excellent. It's good that you've come. We're short-staffed here. The work's not that difficult — it's just a question of application. That's all there is to it. Anyway, you did a pretty good job where you used to be, wouldn't you agree?"

Lin sensed an element of sarcasm in the praise. He

nervously shook his head, "I didn't do much of a job really."

A faint smile flickered across Liu's irregular features and his eyes gleamed shrewdly: "Of course, it might not always be easy. The work we do here is very important. A comrade in the Central Party Committee once said that it is organization work that keeps the Party running smoothly and that without it the Party would have no strength." He continued: "And what does running smoothly mean? It means developing and strengthening the Party, enlarging Party organization and increasing its fighting ability, building a firm foundation for the Party on the basis of collective leadership, criticism and self-criticism and establishing close ties with the masses. As long as we do a better job in this way the Party organization can become strong, vigorous and militant enough to effect reconstruction and transformation ever more successfully."

A dry cough accompanied each sentence, and as he reeled off the well-worked phrases, his speech became faster and faster. When he said "building a firm foundation for the Party", it almost sounded like "building a firm foundation for blah, blah, blah". He was manipulating ideas Lin considered profound and complex like someone deftly using an abacus. Despite deploying all of his powers of concentration, Lin still found himself unable to grasp the full meaning of the words.

Liu then assigned Lin his duties.

As Lin opened the door to leave, Liu stopped him and asked in a casual manner:

"Well then, young Lin, have you got yourself a girl-friend?"

"No. . . ."   Lin blushed.

"Blushing at your age?"   Liu laughed.   "You're only twenty-two.   You've still got plenty of time.   By the way, what's that book in your pocket?"

Lin took out the book and showed him.   Its title was *The Tractor Station Manager and the Chief Agronomist*.

Taking the book, Liu scanned a few lines before asking: "This is the kind of thing that the Youth League recommends you young people to read, isn't it?"

Lin nodded.

"Can I borrow it?"

"Do you get the time to read novels?"   Lin, startled, looked at the pile of papers on his desk.

Liu weighed the book in his hand, "What do you mean?   I can get through this in an evening.   It only took me a week to finish all four volumes of *And Quiet Flows the Don*.   Nothing to it!"

The sky had begun to clear as Lin made for the main organization department office and the few remaining clouds were ringed with light.   Sunlight filled the District Party Committee courtyard.   The place was a hive of activity; a comrade in army uniform, a briefcase under his arm, hurried by; Lu, the gateman, was carrying two large kettles over to the meeting room.   Lin could hear a female voice snapping into the telephone, "No, that won't do.   It has to be by tomorrow at the very latest."   From elsewhere came the sound of sporadic bursts of typing.   Lin wondered if she had just been transferred too.   Without knowing why, he assumed the typist was a woman.   He stood for a while in the hall corridor looking at the sunny

District Party Committee courtyard, relishing the prospect of the new life ahead of him.

2

Including Lin, the organization department had a staff of twenty-four. Three had been temporarily transferred to another department responsible for dealing with counter-revolutionaries, one worked only half-days while preparing for university entrance exams, and another was on maternity leave, leaving only nineteen full-time workers. Of these, four were in charge of cadre work, and the other fifteen were on Party administration and recruitment work in factories, schools and offices. Lin Zhen was assigned to liaise with the No. 2 Factory over the recruitment work of its Party branch.

Because the head of the department, Li Zongqin, was also deputy secretary of the District Party Committee and rarely directly concerned himself with the department's affairs, most of the work in fact fell on First Deputy Head Liu Shiwu's shoulders. Another deputy head was in charge of cadre work. Lin Zhen was directly under Han Changxin, the chief of the section dealing with Party recruitment work in factories.

Han Changxin was very different from Liu Shiwu. Twenty-seven years old, he always wore an immaculate blue navy uniform and his impressive stature matched his handsome, if slightly acne-scarred, features. Patting Lin on the back and interjecting the occasional hearty laugh as he outlined his duties, Han seemed more like a leading cadre than the real thing.

This impression was reinforced in the office the next day when Lin saw him talking with a Party branch member in charge of organization.

"Why did you only spend half an hour talking to them? I told you over the phone that you'd need at least two hours to discuss the recruitment plan!"

"But we've just been too busy at the factory this month. . . ."

Han cut in sharply: "So does this mean that recruitment gets pushed to one side if the factory is busy? That's tantamount to pitting ideological work against regular work and means that the Party would be neglecting its own affairs."

Lin didn't know what he meant. He was more familiar with phrases like "the five key links in the classroom" and "audio-visual aids in teaching". He admired Han's vision and ability, the smooth way in which he was able to see the principles involved in an issue and to direct others.

At this point, Lin turned his head and saw Zhao Huiwen bent over the table copying out some papers. Looking up quizzically at Han Changxin, she adjusted her amber-coloured hairclips before turning to gaze pensively out of the window.

That evening, after some of the cadres had gone out to take part in branch level activities and others were resting, Zhao Huiwen continued copying out a document entitled "The Successful Experience of the Sub-bureau of Taxation in Training and Promoting Cadres". Her wrist ached after a long day's work and she frequently stopped to shake it and blow on it. Lin volunteered to give her a hand, but she refused saying: "Thank you, but I think I'd better do it my-

self really." So instead Lin helped to put the finished
papers in order and hovered beside her, trying to give
the impression of being useful. Every now and then
she would look up at him from her work until finally
he asked: "What do you keep on looking at me for?"
Zhao just nibbled the end of her pen and laughed.

3

Lin Zhen had graduated from a teachers college in
the autumn of 1953. At that time he had been a pro-
bationary Party member and was assigned to teach at
the principal primary school in the district. Despite
his new job, he continued leading the life of a student:
in the mornings he worked out with weights and every
evening he would write in his diary. Before every
national holiday he would conscientiously solicit
others' opinions of his behaviour. Some people pre-
dicted that within three months he would fall into
some of the less exemplary habits of adult life. Before
long however, many of his colleagues commented fa-
vourably on his dedication, saying that nothing seemed to distract him from his work.

And Lin didn't disappoint them. During the 1954
winter break, he even received an award for his work
from the Bureau of Education.

It might have been assumed that this young
teacher's existence was a perfectly content and stable
one. But this was not the case, for even someone as
seemingly uncomplicated as Lin Zhen had his own anxieties.

A year later, Lin was making even greater demands

on himself. Was the stimulus the impetus of the high tide of socialism, was it a response to the call made at the National Youth Socialist Activists Conference or was it simply that he was getting older?

He was already twenty-two and he remembered how, in the first grade of junior middle school, he had written an essay entitled: *When I Am Twenty-two.*

Now he had reached that age, yet his life still seemed to be a blank page, undistinguished by any achievement, creation, adventure, untouched even by love. In fact he had never even so much as written to a girl. Certainly he worked hard but he had achieved little when compared with the young activists and it was no comfort to him to realize how fast life was flying by. He made ambitious plan to study and wanted to conquer the world in a day.

And now, with his new job, it seemed that perhaps his real life was beginning and that his essay could have read "When I am twenty-two I shall be a Party worker". He had suppressed his reluctance to leave his school and his young pupils and had become fired with enthusiasm for his new job. After he had had a talk with his branch secretary, he had lain awake thinking the whole night.

And so it was with a sense of jubilation that he climbed the steps of the District Party Committee offices with a copy of *The Tractor Station Manager and the Chief Agronomist* in his pocket, full of fervent anticipation of the life he would lead as a Party worker (though in fact his conception of this was based entirely on the impression of capable and all-powerful Party secretaries he'd gained from films). But when he finally did come face-to-face with the busy, self-possessed leading cadres, the documents and the meetings, the sharp quarrels and exhaustive analyses, he blinked his light brown eyes and felt somewhat disconcerted. . . .

On his fourth day at the District Party Committee, Lin went to the Tonghua Gunny Sack Factory to assess party recruitment work during the first quarter of the year. Before going, he read the relevant documents and a pamphlet entitled *Investigation and Research Procedures*. After repeatedly consulting Han Changxin, he prepared a detailed outline, and then raced off to the factory on his recently-acquired bicycle.

On hearing that he was a cadre from the District Party Committee, the factory security guard allowed him to enter without having to register. He walked across an empty yard, past a hemp storage shed and a noisy machine shop, and then nervously knocked on the office door of the factory manager and Party branch secretary, Wang Qingquan. "Come in," said a voice. He entered slowly, afraid that moving quickly might reveal his inexperience. He saw a small, broad-faced man playing chess with a hunchbacked greasy-haired partner. The small man looked up, moved a chess piece with his right hand, and after finding out who Lin wanted to see, waved his arm impatiently: "Go and talk to Wei Heming in the Party branch office in the west wing. He's in charge of organizational work." With this he lowered his head and resumed the game.

Lin found the ruddy-complexioned Wei and proceeded to ask questions based on his prepared outline. "How may people have you recruited during the first quarter of 1956?"

"One and a half," he replied gruffly.

"What do you mean 'half'?"

"Approval's come through from the District Party Committee for one but we've been waiting on the other for more than two months now."

Lin drew out his notebook and started writing.

"Can you give me an idea how you go about recruiting people here?"

"The same as always — in line with the Party constitution."

Lin looked at him, wondering why he sounded as dry as a week-old corn bread. Wei rested his chin on his hand and looked away, seemingly preoccupied.

Lin asked again: "So what have been the results of the recruitment work?"

"I've just told you. What else is there to say?" Wei replied, obviously wishing to get the discussion over and done with as soon as possible.

Lin, disconcerted, didn't know what to ask next. He'd spent a whole afternoon preparing an outline only to find his interview was over in five minutes.

Just at that moment the door was flung open and in came the small chess-playing comrade. "Have you heard about that letter?" he demanded.

Wei nodded perfunctorily.

The man paced up and down before firmly positioning himself in the centre of the room: "You people have got to do something about this. This quality control problem was brought up last year, so why have you waited for the contractor to write to the textile ministry? It's absolutely shameful when the whole nation is putting its energies into socialist reconstruction that we can't speed up our production!"

"Just who are you talking about?" Wei's voice shook with anger as he glared at the small man.

"I'm talking about the lot of you!" He made a sweeping gesture, encompassing Lin.

Wei, making a strenuous effort to control his anger, became even more flushed. He stood up and asked: "And what about your good self? Don't you have any responsibility in this?"

"Of course I have," replied the small man coolly. "My responsibility is to my superiors and I'm prepared to accept any disciplinary measures they might feel necessary. As for you, you're answerable to me. After all you are the production chief. You'd better be careful. . . ." He threw Wei a menacing look and walked out.

Sitting down, Wei took a deep breath and unbuttoned his padded jacket.

"Who was that?" Lin asked.

"You mean you didn't recognize him?" Wei's tone was sarcastic. "That's Wang Qingquan, the factory manager."

Wei proceeded to fill Lin in on Wang Qingquan. As a result of some involvement with a woman, he'd been transferred to the factory as deputy manager in 1951. In 1953, the manager was moved elsewhere and Wang took over the job. Since then he'd spent most of his time swaggering around the workshops and other offices, occasionally hiding himself in his office writing instructions on documents or playing chess, and then every month at union meetings, party branch meetings and Youth League meetings would make speeches criticizing the workers for not having a competitive enough attitude, for not paying enough attention to quality, for having capitalist tendencies and so on. Before Wei had finished speaking, Wang came in again. He looked at his watch and ordered: "Notify all the leading comrades of the Party, Youth League, Union and administrative sections to meet in my office at ten past twelve." With this he left, slamming the door behind him.

"You can see what kind of person he is," Wei murmured.

"Why don't you criticize him instead of sitting around grumbling. Report him to the higher-ups. There's no way that a factory manager like that would be allowed."

"You must be new around here, Comrade Lin," said Wei with a smile.

"Comrade Lin" blushed.

"Criticizing him wouldn't make any difference. How can you criticize the man when he hardly even attends Party meetings. Even if he does turn up and you say something he just comes out with things like 'Of course it's important to express opinions. However you should always have a sense of propriety and choose the correct occasion. We can't waste the Party's time on individual concerns when there are vital national issues to be discussed.' Fair enough. But if I try not to waste any of that precious time and bring it up privately, the result is what you've just seen."

"Have you reported this?"

"In 1954 I wrote letters to the Ministry of Textiles and to the District Party Committee and as a result they sent a Comrade Zhang from the ministry and your colleague Han to investigate. Their findings were, and I quote: 'The degree of bureaucratism in this factory is comparatively serious but the primary problem is one of work style. Fundamentally the declared objectives are realised but the approach does have its shortcomings.' So they criticized Wang and gave me a general pep talk encouraging a 'healthy approach towards the criticism of one's seniors' and that was that. For about a month or so afterwards he was relatively conscientious but then he came down with a kidney ailment. When he'd recovered he said he'd developed the illness due to pressure of work and went back to his old ways."

"Report him again then."

"Ha! I don't know how many times I brought it up with Han Changxin but all he did was come out with the same old lecture about respecting one's leaders and strengthening unity. Perhaps I'm wrong but sometimes it seems almost as though Wang will have to become an embezzler or a rapist before any of the higher-ups takes any notice!"

Frowning, Lin made his return journey at a considerably slower pace. His first assignment had not been easy but it had presented him with a challenge, a real chance to prove his mettle. He remained lost in thought until pulled up by a reprimand from a policeman for riding in the fast lane.

4

As soon as he finished lunch, Lin rushed off to report to Han Changxin. He rested his solid, almost cumbersome frame wearily against the sofa. He started picking his teeth with a match.

Lin gave him a disjointed account of his visit to the factory. Tapping his foot, Han replied: "Yes, yes, I know." He patted him on the shoulder and said cheerfully: "Don't worry. This is only your first time. You can't expect to understand everything all at once. Next time it'll be better."

"Yes, but I know all I need to know about Wang Qingquan already." Lin opened his notebook.

Reaching over, Han shut the notebook: "I know all about it too. The year before last the District Party Committee sent me to look into the situation. I criticized him severely, pointing out his shortcomings and telling him what grave consequences they'd have. We must have talked for at least three or four hours. . . ."

"But it obviously didn't have any effect. Wei said it only took a month before he. . . ." Lin interrupted.

"A month is better than nothing, but in fact it's been more than that. It's not as if Wei doesn't have his problems too. The moment he sees someone he starts complaining about Wang. . . ."

"But aren't his complaints valid?"

"Difficult to say for sure one way or another. Of course this problem has to be sorted out. I've already talked about it with Comrade Li Zongqin, the District Party Committee Deputy Secretary."

"And what did he have to say?"

"He feels the way I do. The problem of Wang can and must be resolved. But it's not a good idea for you to get too caught up in all this so quickly."

"Really?"

"Yes. This was your first assignment and you couldn't possibly get the full picture all at once.

What's more it isn't your job to solve the problem of Wang Qingquan anyway. To be frank, to do that would take somebody a lot more experienced than you. After all, it's not as if we haven't been dealing with it. If you just dive headlong into all of this, it would take you at least three months to see it through and you wouldn't have time to get to grips with the first quarter's Party recruitment. They're chasing us to hand in a report as it is!"

Lin was silent.

"Don't get so worked up." Han patted him on the shoulder again. "We've got three thousand Party members and over a hundred branches in the district. How can you expect to cope with our problems when you've just arrived?" He yawned. "Time for a nap."

"But just how are you supposed to carry out recruitment work?" Lin asked helplessly.

He dodged away as Han made to pat him on the shoulder again. Han responded reassuringly: "How about if we go there together tomorrow and I'll give you some help?" With this he shepherded Lin in the direction of the dormitory.

It was with great interest that Lin watched to see how Han handled things the following day. On teaching practice three years ago when he was a student at the Beijing Teachers College he'd gained a great deal by watching an experienced teacher at work in the classroom. He saw this as much the same sort of opportunity. He opened his notebook in readiness to take detailed notes on Han's methods.

Han began by asking Wei: "How many new Party members have you recruited in the first quarter?"

"One and a half."

It's not one and a half. It's two." corrected Han. "I didn't come here to find out whether they've been passed by the District Party Committee or not. I came to check what progress you've been making with recruitment work." He continued: "How have these two done with regard to this quarter's production plan?"

"Fine. One of them has exceeded the quota by seven percent, the other by four. Both have been publicly commended by the factory. . . ."

Wei displayed a degree of enthusiasm when discussing the factory's productivity but Han cut him short: "What about their shortcomings?"

After some thought Wei trotted out one or two minor examples.

Han asked him to be more specific.

Han then went on to ask him again about the performance of Party activists for this quarter, paying particular attention to facts and figures. He seemed to have little interest, however, in hearing about ways in which they had overcome difficulties to introduce innovations.

On his return, Han, in a practised hand, wrote out a specimen report entitled "Recruitment Work at the Gunny Sack Factory" which read as follows:

During the quarter under discussion (January-March 1956), the Gunny Sack Factory's Party branch effected a positive and prudent plan for Party recruitment, and in this respect made certain achievements in Party building work. New Party members Zhu and Fan, spurred on by the glorious title of Party member and reinforced by their sense of being masters of their own affairs, exceeded their substantial production quotas in the first quarter by 7% and 4% respectively. The broad mass of activists rallied around the Party branch and, educated by the model example of Zhu and Fan and encouraged by their determination to join the Party, brought into play their initiative and creativity and splendidly met or exceeded their production tasks for this quarter (this was followed by a series of figures and concrete examples) . . . this illustrates that not only is Party building work not contradict production work but that it provides an enormous impetus to production, and that the practice of neglecting Party work using production pressure as an excuse is mistaken. At the same time, it must be pointed out that Party building work at the Gunny Sack Factory still has certain shortcomings. . . . For example. . . ,

Lin read and reread the report, wondering whether or not he had actually even been to the factory or whether he'd perhaps been asleep during his visit with Han. How else could he account for having forgotten so much? Baffled, he asked Han:

"What's all this based on?"

"On Wei's report that day."

"You think that their production successes are a result of Party building work?" Lin stammered.

Han brushed a trouser leg, "Of course."

"Surely not. He never said anything like that. Maybe their increase in production was the result of a competition, or perhaps because the Youth League set up a production supervisory post.   Anyway it's not necessarily anything to do with Party work. . . ."

"Oh, that I don't deny.   But it's all interrelated. You can't really say that one factor is more important than another."

"But if we were writing a report on the first quarter's rat-catching results, would we use the same kind of statistics and framework?"

Wei smiled indulgently at Lin's naivete.   "You have to be a little flexible and use strategy. . . ."

"But how did you know their production quotas were high?" persisted Lin.

"Surely all factories have high quotas these days."

Lin was speechless.

5

Lin's first ten days in his new job were to produce a host of impressions and questions, far more than his two years at the primary school had ever done. Work at the District Party Committee was solemn and tense with endless meetings lasting until late in the evening. From the Chinese Phonetic Alphabet to the prevention of encephalitis, from labour protection to lectures on political economy, all fell within the scope of the District Party Committee's work.   Once when Lin went to the postroom to collect the newspapers, he came across an awesomely thick document entitled: "Report Submitted for Instructions by the Party Group of the District People's Committee on Revising the Distribution, Administration and Management of the Joint State-private Industrial and Commercial Enterprises and on Implementing the Decision of the Municipal Party Committee Concerning Wage Scales in Joint State-private Industrial and Commercial Enterprises". At times, looking around, one might gain the impression that the District Party Committee cadres spent all their time taking it easy, chatting or reading newspapers and even joking about subjects Lin Zhen considered to be sacrosanct.   Once, for example, when talking about the supervisory posts set up by Youth League members, Han Changxin's reaction was to say half-mockingly: "Hey, those kids have really worked at it this time. . . ."   A discussion on Party work assigned by the Municipal Party Committee proved a revelation to Lin. Everyone sat around smoking, talking and laughing, and the meeting dragged on for two hours with no visible results until Liu Shiwu, who until then sat silently thinking, produced a scheme which immediately sparked off an animated discussion.   Lin was filled with admiration at the number of stimulating points raised and felt that the last thirty minutes of the discussion seemed ten times more stimulating than the previous two hours.   Some evenings there would be a light on in every room.   In the Number One Meeting Room there would be cordial discussions between portly businessmen and the United Front department chief.   In the Number Two Meeting Room, the political study aides from each unit would be battling over the definitions of 'price' and 'value'. Excited young applicants to join the Party would be awaiting their first interviews in the Organization Department or the chief and deputy secretary of the District Party Committee would be giving a report on the implementation of wage reform to a stern-faced secretary from the Municipal Party Committee on an unscheduled visit. At times like this, with the general hubbub and people dashing back and forth and telephones ringing incessantly, it seemed to Lin that he could feel the throbbing pulse of the whole district and that the pedestrian old courtyard was transformed.

And in all of this, the person who made the strongest impression on him was Liu Shiwu. Despite the fact that Liu had a heavy work load, often with simultaneous phone calls urging him to attend meetings, he still managed to finish reading *The Tractor Station Manager and the Chief Agronomist* before passing it on to Han Changxin. On top of this, he had even learned the Draft Scheme for the Chinese Phonetic Alphabet issued only a month previously and was even beginning to use it to make notes during meetings. He would scan the titles and conclusions of some documents before signing his name and passing them on, while taking a whole afternoon to read and make notes on much shorter ones. Sometimes, while Han Changxin was reporting to him on the current situation, he would be glancing through papers and then suddenly exclaim: "It was't like that the last time you reported!" Han would force a smile as Liu scrutinized him, but usually Liu would pursue the matter no further and return to his reading while Han regained his composure and continued with his report.

There was something in the relationship between Zhao Huiwen and Han Changxin that caught Lin's attention. Han was a habitual back-slapper. It was only with Zhao that he kept a professional distance. And Zhao in her turn maintained a businesslike and somewhat guarded attitude towards Han.

It was April and a mild east wind was blowing. Heating stoves were no longer needed and had been put away in a dark storeroom. All that remained to remind people of the harsh winter were the dark patches of soot on the ceiling of each room. In years past, Lin used to take groups of children to the Sleeping Buddha Temple or Badachu in the Western Hills looking for signs of spring in the newly-opened peach and plum blossoms and muddy streams. Life at the District Party Committee, however, remained virtually untouched by the changing of the seasons, continuing as always in its complex and intense perambulations. Lin plucked a plump, tender willow bud in the courtyard and experienced a slight sense of depression. Spring had come so fast, yet he had done nothing worth mentioning to meet this most beautiful of seasons. . . .

At nine one evening Lin went to Liu Shiwu's office. Zhao Huiwen was there wearing a dark purple pullover, her face pale in the electric light. Hearing Lin enter, she turned around and he saw traces of tears on her high cheekbones. He turned to go but Liu Shiwu, head lowered and smoking, motioned to him to stay: "Sit down. We've almost finished talking."

Lin went to sit in a dimly lit corner and began reading a newspaper. Describing circles in the air with his cigarette, Liu continued in earnest:

"Take it from me. I know what I'm talking about. You young people are all alike. At first you only see the good things and think it's all a bed of roses, then you gradually discover one another's faults and come down to earth with a bump. You shouldn't be so unreasonable. He hasn't abandoned or mistreated you

and there are no problems about his political or moral
character, so how can you say you can't go on any
longer? It's been only four years after all. You've
been seeing too many foreign films, that's all there
is to it. . . ."

Zhao Huiwen said nothing. Flicking back her hair
with her hand, she gave Lin a wan smile as she left.

Liu turned to Lin, "How's everything going?" He
threw his cigarette end to the ground and lit another,
puffing greedily before blowing out a slow stream of
smoke. "Zhao's fallen out with her husband again."
He opened the window. A gust of wind blew some
papers from his desk and carried in the sounds of
laughter and bicycle bells from the front courtyard as
a meeting broke up.

Liu threw away his half-smoked cigarette. He
stretched, leaned against the windowsill and said in
a low voice, "Spring really is here."

"I want to talk about working at the District Party
Committee. There are a few things I don't know how
to deal with," said Lin resolutely, gathering up papers
from the floor as he spoke.

"Fine. Good. Carry on," Liu replied, still leaning
against the windowsill.

Lin began with his visit to the sack factory: "When
I went into the factory manager's office, I saw Wang
Qingquan. . . ."

"Was he playing chess or poker at the time?" Liu
asked with a slight smile.

"How did you know?" Lin asked, startled.

"I have a pretty fair idea what he's up to most of
the time," Liu said slowly. "He's a real chess addict.
Once, when we were halfway through a meeting he

disappeared off to the toilet. When he didn't return I went out to look for him and there he was watching Old Lu and the district secretary's son playing chess. He was standing on the sidelines throwing in his two cents every now and then."

Ignoring Liu's casual interruption, Lin continued by relaying Wei Heming's complaints about Wang.

Liu Shiwu closed the window, pulled up a chair and sat down. He leaned forward slightly, his hands on his knees, and shook his head:

"Wei is a fairly outspoken type. From the moment he arrived he started arguing bitterly with Wang Qingquan. As for Wang himself, he's not as simple as he might appear. After the anti-Japanese war he was sent to work in the Kuomintang army where he became a deputy regimental commander. He was one of our best intelligence agents. He lost contact with us from 1947 until after Liberation. His job was to undermine the enemy but in the process he picked up a few of their bad habits, which he's failed to correct. All the same he's really a fine old comrade."

"If that's the case. . . ."

"It is." Liu nodded solemnly. "Of course, this isn't meant to be a speech in his defence. After all, the Party sent him to fight the enemy, not to be contaminated by them, so his mistakes are unforgivable."

"But how can they be corrected? Wei Heming said that this is a long-standing problem. He's written letters all over the place. . . ."

"That's right." Liu Shiwu coughed drily and went on, gesturing: "There are all kinds of problems at the branch level at the moment. If you try and solve them all individually, you would be wasting your energies with little or no result. What's more, we're always being chased to get on with other jobs. It's difficult enough to get anything done as it is. A leader must be able to integrate specific and general issues and learn the art of balancing priorities between assignments from above and problems at the grassroots level. It's true that Wang is not a hard worker but he isn't exactly a slacker either. He does have a rather rigid work style but he hasn't actually violated any regulations yet. So I think it's not a question of formally disciplining him so much as putting him back on the right track. It seems to me though that it's not yet the right time to deal with this particular problem."

Lin Zhen was silent. It seemed as though two options lay before him: He could either follow Nastya's principle of nipping transgressions in the bud or he could fall in with Liu's policy of waiting until the time was ripe. He was unable to think of people like Wang being factory managers without feeling a little uncomfortable, but at the same time he was unable to refute Liu Shiwu's ideas on the art of leadership. Liu added: "Actually there are plenty more like him."

This statement, so much at variance with the Party lectures he had attended at the primary school, astounded Lin.

He went on to recount the discrepancies between Han Changxin's report and what he himself had actually witnessed, saying that the report had not been a very truthful reflection.

Liu burst out laughing and said, "Trust him. He's a clever one." He sighed and went on. "Alright. I'll tell him what you think."

Lin stood up hesitantly.

"Anything else?" asked Liu.

Mustering his courage, Lin exclaimed: "I don't know why but ever since I arrived I seem to keep coming up against problems. I never thought Party leadership organizations would be like this. . . ."

Liu put down his cup. "Of course it's always good to have imagination but real life is rather different. It's not a question of whether or not there are any shortcomings so much as which ones are paramount. Taking the District Party Committee's work as a whole, including our department, would you say our successes outweighed our failures? Of course they do, and our problems are the kind that occur as advances are being made. Our great undertaking is carried out by precisely these very same imperfect organizations and Party members."

Lin felt a little odd after leaving the office: Talking with Liu Shiwu should have settled some of his doubts but instead he felt that his ideas had been thrown into even greater confusion.

6

Not long afterwards, Lin Zhen received severe criticism at a meeting of his Party section.

It came about this way: On one of his visits to the gunny sack factory Lin was told by Wei Heming that Wang had given the workers a telling-off because the production quality targets had not been achieved. This had produced a strong reaction, in response to which Wei Heming was planning to hold a meeting to hear the opinions of the workers and to report the findings to the higher-ups. Lin had been very much in favour of the move, feeling that perhaps it would help stimulate "the ripening of conditions". Three days later, Wang Qingquan, in a state of panic, rushed to the District Party Committee to find the assistant secretary, Li Zongqin, claiming that Wei Heming, with the support of Lin Zhen, was organizing a clique against the leadership. He also said that the workers at Wei's meeting all had "bad records" and finished by declaring that he wanted to resign. Li criticized a few of his shortcomings and agreed to stop Wei from holding any further meetings. "As for Lin Zhen," he said to Wang, "we'll see that he gets the education that he needs."

At the meeting Han delivered his analysis of the situation: "Lin Zhen did not consult the leadership on the matter, but agreed without authorization to allow Wei to convene the meeting in question. This is irregular and undisciplined behaviour. . . ."

Lin himself remained unconvinced: "Of course I'm at fault for not consulting the leadership. But I still don't understand why we don't attempt to find out what the masses are thinking and even prevent moves in this direction!"

"Who says we don't understand?" retorted Han. "We have a very good grasp of the situation at the sack factory."

"To grasp the situation and not solve it is what really upsets me. The Party Constitution says that Party members should oppose anything that is not in the Party's interests. . . ." Lin's face grew dark.

At this point the experienced Liu Shiwu interrupted, as always taking the initiative at a critical juncture.

"Comrade Lin's enthusiasm for his work is commendable. However it is rather presumptuous of him to give a lecture on the Party Constitution to the cadres of the organization department when he's only been here a month. He is obviously under the impression that he is supporting criticism from below and doing a good thing and he certainly has the best of motives. However all moves to criticize the leadership must originate with the leadership. Now let's just ask Comrade Lin Zhen to think about the situation a bit. Firstly, is it not the case that Wei has a personal prejudice against Wang Qingquan? That would be hard to deny.   And when Wei organises a meeting with such enthusiasm, could it not be for personal motives? I think that's not entirely out of the question. Secondly, could it also not be suggested that the people attending this meeting had complex personal backgrounds and ulterior motives?   We should also take this into account.   Thirdly, wouldn't holding a meeting like this give the masses the erroneous impression that Wang Qingquan will be dealt with very soon, thus creating confusion among the masses? And so on.   As far as Lin Zhen is concerned, I'm willing to offer my honest opinion.   Young people are really prone to idealizing life.   He thinks that life should conform to his ideal, but a Party worker has to be more realistic than that.   Young people have a very high opinion of themselves and plenty of ambition. When they start a new job they think they can battle against all the shortcomings, like Nastya, the heroine in the novel. This is laudable and heartwarming but it's also based on wishful thinking. . . ."

Lin Zhen felt almost as though someone had hit him and bit his bottom lip hard.

With a final touch of bravado he asked, "What about Wang Qingquan. . . ?" Liu Shiwu raised his head. "I'm going to have a talk with him tomorrow. You're not the only one around here who has principles."

7

Han Changxin's wedding was on Saturday night. Lin went to the reception but found that he didn't like the choking thick smoke, the wrappers and fruit peel littering the floor, nor the boisterous atmosphere. Without even waiting for the ceremony to begin he left.

It was dark in the organization department office. He turned on the light and spotted a letter lying on his desk. It was from his colleagues at the primary school, and also contained a letter from his ex-pupils.

"Dear Teacher Lin: How are you? We miss you very, very much. After you left all the girls cried and then we did some very, very difficult sums. It was such hard work, but we finally got it rite in the end. . . ."

Reading the letter, Lin couldn't help smiling to himself. He changed "rite" to "right" thinking that he should tell them to be more careful with their spelling next time they wrote. He pictured delicate little Li Linlin with a bow in her hair, Liu Xiaomao who liked to paint and Meng Fei who was always chewing the end of his pencil. . . . With a start he raised his head but all he could see was the telephone, some blotting paper and his glass-topped desk. The children's world with which he had been so familiar and his former, far less complex job were already behind him now. He thought back to the criticism of the day before. Could it be that he'd really been wrong? Had it really been so impetuous and naive, just the effortless courage of youth? Perhaps he should think it through a bit more, and in the meantime just get on with his own job. Maybe in a couple of years, when he had "ripened" a little, he would be able to confront such issues again.

The sound of laughter and loud noises erupted from the auditorium.

Lin turned around with a start when a hand fell on his shoulder. The light hurt his eyes. Zhao Huiwen was standing quietly beside him and he thought to himself that women seemed to have an innate ability to move silently.

"Why aren't you at the wedding?" she asked.

"Oh, I don't feel like it. What about you?"

"I should be getting on home," she replied. "Why don't you come over to my place for a while? At least you won't have to sit around moping."

"Oh, I'm not really," disputed Lin. He appreciated her thoughtfulness though and accepted.

Zhao Huiwen lived in a small courtyard not far from the District Party Committee.

Her son lay asleep in a light blue cot sucking his thumb. Zhao kissed him and then took Lin into the other room.

"His father isn't back yet?" asked Lin.

Zhao shook her head.

The room looked as though it had been decorated in a hurry. Its bare walls were stark white. A washstand stood in one corner and a vase gaped emptily on the windowsill. Only the radio on the bedside table seemed capable of breaking the room's silence.

Lin sat in a rattan chair while Zhao stood leaning against the wall. He pointed at the vase: "You ought to get some flowers to go in that," he said, "and why don't you put up a few pictures."

"Since I'm hardly ever here, it doesn't seem that important," replied Zhao. "Would you like to listen to the radio? They always have good music on Saturday nights."

She turned on the radio and a dreamy, gentle melody drifted through the room.

Its tempo gradually increasing, the violin's lyrical theme moved Lin a great deal. He rested his chin in his hand and listened raptly. The melody seemed to contain his youth, all his aspirations and frustrations.

Zhao continued leaning against the wall, heedless of the whitewash rubbing off on her clothes. When the music finished she said in a melodious voice: "This is Tchaikovsky's *Capriccio Italien*. It makes me think of the south, of the sea. . . . I used to listen to it when I was working in the cultural troupe. Ultimately it came to seem almost as though it was springing directly from my own heart."

"You were in a cultural troupe?"

"I was sent there after being at a military academy. I don't have a very good voice but I used to sing for the troops in Korea."

Lin looked at Zhao Huiwen as if for the first time.

"Don't you think I look like a singer?" The music had been replaced by a drama broadcast and Zhao reached over and turned it off.

"If you used to belong to a cultural troupe, why do you hardly ever sing?"

Making no reply she walked over to the bed and sat down. "I'd like to have a talk with you. Tell me, what do you think of the District Party Committee?"

"I don't really know. I haven't really worked out exactly what I think yet."

"I get the feeling you've got your own ideas about Liu Shiwu and Han Changxin. Am I right?"

"Perhaps."

"I used to be like that too. It took me a long time to get used to things here after the discipline of the army. After I arrived I came out with a lot of suggestions and had a real set-to with Han Changxin. But I just got laughed at for being naive and they accused me of launching into a whole load of complaints before even doing my own job properly. Gradually I began to realize that I wasn't up to waging a battle against what I saw as shortcomings. . . ."

"Why not?" Lin jumped up in agitation.

"It was all my own fault." She grabbed a pillow and rested it on her knees. "I felt very inexperienced and inadequate and by no means justified in taking issue with comrades more experienced than myself. Actually it's not as if Liu Shiwu, Han Changxin and the others don't generally do a good job. Their faults are scattered through their achievements like dust in the air. In fact they're almost intangible. You know

they're there but you can't put your finger on them.
That's the real problem."

"You're so right!" Lin smacked his fist against his
palm.

Zhao, finding herself caught up in his mood, threw
aside the pillow and said slowly: "All I do is routine
work. The leadership doesn't concern itself much with
it. And then there's my private life. I keep myself to
myself — just copy out things, then go home and wash
nappies and buy milk powder. I feel I'm getting old
fast. I don't know what happened to the dreams and
the enthusiasm I used to have when I was at the
military academy." She fell silent and sat playing
with her fingers. Finally she continued: "Two months
ago, Beijing entered the 'high tide of socialism' and
everybody started celebrating. All the workers and
shop assistants and even capitalists set off firecrackers
and went to the District Party Committee beating
gongs and drums welcoming the good news. Many of
them applied directly to the organization department
to join the Party. So many things were happening.
The entire District Party Committee used to sit up
all night. At mealtimes, comrades from the propaganda
department and the finance department used to talk
non-stop about everything that was going on. But
what did we do? It didn't really affect our department at all. All we did was make a few telephone
calls pushing for new recruitment figures, and write
a summary by adding a few more examples here and
there to last year's forms. There's been a move recently to get people to be more vigilant about con-
servative thinking. The organization department's
contribution was to hold three sloppy meetings, write

a report and leave it at that. Oh, I don't know what I'm saying really, but it was like every time I heard a firecracker going off I felt inspired. Whenever I copied out the names of new Party members, my hand was trembling with excitement. But can we really go on in this way?" She sighed and paced back and forth. "When I said what I thought at the Party section meeting Han just looked pleased with himself and said, 'Aren't our recruiting figures the highest of all the districts? And what's more, hasn't the Municipal Party Committee's organization department asked us to present a summary of our experiences?' Then he started analysing me directly saying that I was being negative because I didn't like the routine work."

"On first meeting Han makes quite an impression on people, but when you really get to know him. . . ." Lin brought up the time Han had written the report.

Zhao nodded. "I haven't said much in the last couple of years but I still keep my eyes open. There are two sides to everything and people can put on a good front. Just look at Han Changxin. He knows how to pull the leader bit by moralizing at other people. He knows the right examples to use when he writes a report and he can come up with the right generalizations when he has to make an analysis. He gets by very nicely by appearing to be on the ball at all times."

"What about Liu Shiwu?" asked Lin. "I think there's a lot more to him. But underneath all his original ideas and penetrating analyses he seems to be frighteningly detached. I don't really know how he can put up with a factory manager like Wang Qingquan. But when I tried to tell him what I thought, his arguments just confused me. It's as if you can only do things his way. . . ."

"Liu's pet phrase is 'that's all there is to it'. He sees through everything, and thinks he's got it all worked out. As he says himself, he knows what's right from what's wrong and that sooner or later right will win out. He's seen it all and he knows it all. You get a lot of experience working for the Party and now it's all routine to him. He doesn't have any strong feelings left either way. If something's a success he's duly appreciative and if something's not right his reaction is just to laugh at it. He feels he knows all he needs to know apart from the occasional special thing like the new romanization system. Once he feels the time is ripe he goes into action and lords it over everybody. Of course with his experience and knowledge there are some things he does do well but that only makes him more full of himself." It was obvious that Zhao had spent many sleepless nights mulling over this.

"What about our assistant district Party secretary-cum-department chief? What does he think about all this?"

Zhao Huiwen became even more animated. "Li Zhongqin's health is not so good. And he complains that District Party Committee work is too mundane, that he'd rather be doing theoretical study. He's only the department's head in name and in reality all the work is done by Liu Shiwu. This kind of thing happens a lot. You get old Party members with titles like factory manager, college head or Party secretary who are either sick, haven't got much of an education or got the job because they're somebody's spouse. But the real work is done by the deputy manager, the vice director or the secretaries."

"And what about our district Party secretary Comrade Zhou Runxiang?"

"Zhou is a very admirable leading comrade who is worthy of great respect, but he is just far too busy dealing with counter-revolutionaries and the reform of private enterprises. All these things call for immediate action unlike the work we do in the organization department, so he doesn't really pay us that much attention."

"But what can we do?" It was only then that the complexity of the situation dawned on Lin.

"That's the question." Zhao, pensive, drummed on her thigh as if playing a piano. She looked away and smiled. "Thank you. . . ."

"Thank me?" Lin Zhen thought he'd misheard.

"Yes. When I see you, I feel young again. You're not afraid of anything. You're prepared to battle for whatever is right. But I've got a woman's instinct for things and for you. . . . There's trouble in the air."

Lin blushed. He'd never thought of himself this way. On the contrary, he felt ashamed at his own ineptitude. "Well, let's hope it's something worth getting your teeth into," he mumbled. "You've obviously been doing an awful lot of thinking about this. Why have you been keeping it all to yourself?"

"I just don't seem to be able to put my finger on anything specific." She folded her arms. "But I'm learning more all the time. Sometimes I can't sleep because I spend all night thinking and then I ask myself how I can possibly understand all these things since all I do is routine office work."

222 The Butterfly and Other Stories

"How can you say that? I think what you've just said is absolutely correct. You ought to tell the District Party secretary what you've just told me or write to the *People's Daily*. . . ."

"Oh, there you go again." She smiled broadly.

"What do you mean?" Upset, Lin stood up, scratching his head. "I've been thinking about this a lot too. It seems to me that you can only correct yourself through struggle. You can't wait until you feel sure you are correct and then begin to struggle."

At that moment Zhao suddenly went out, leaving Lin alone in the large room. He could smell soap. Just as suddenly she returned, skipping like a little girl, and carrying a long-handled pot. Removing the lid she said with a flourish:

"Look I've got some boiled water chestnuts. They're the only good thing I've got in the house."

Delighted, Lin took the pot from her and said, "I've loved these ever since I was little!" He bit into a large, unpeeled one and then suddenly spat it out. "This one's bad! It tastes absolutely horrible!" Zhao roared with laughter as he threw the rest to the ground in disgust.

When Lin made to go it was late and flickering stars filled the vast clear sky. They heard an old vendor crying out: "Meatballs! Nice hot meatballs!" Lin stood outside and Zhao remained framed in the doorway, her eyes shining in the darkness. "Next time you come there'll be pictures on the wall."

Lin smiled warmly: "I hope you'll take up singing again too!" He shook her hand and left.

Breathing deeply, he savoured the fragrant spring night air and felt a new warmth inside.

8

Han Changxin had just been appointed deputy director of the organization department. This and his recent marriage had made him even more energetic. He shaved every day and got himself a new woollen suit made after visiting a garment exhibition. However he spent more time in the office hearing reports, correcting documents or talking with people, and less time working outside. Liu Shiwu was as busy as ever.

After supper one evening Han Changxin returned *The Tractor Station Manager and the Chief Agronomist* to Lin. Patting the book, he said, "Very interesting but a bit preposterous. It's not bad being a writer — you can make up as much as you like. One of these days when I've got rheumatism or have been kicked out for making a mistake, I'll go off and write a novel."

Lin quickly opened a drawer and placed the book at the bottom.

Liu Shiwu, who was sitting in a nearby armchair pondering the final moves in a chess game, overheard Han and said sarcastically: "It's not impossible that old Han will have rheumatism or be punished, but as for writing a novel, I think we can rest assured it's unlikely that we'll ever see a masterpiece from him on this planet." The acidity of his comment made Han awkwardly turn his head away pretending he hadn't heard.

Liu called Lin Zhen over and motioned to him to sit down. "What have you been reading recently? Any new books to lend me?"

Lin shook his head.

Leaning back against the sofa, hands behind his

head and eyes half shut, Liu said in a leisurely fashion: "Not so long ago I read *Virgin Soil* which was serialized in *Translation* magazine. It's very well written, very lively."

"Do you often read novels?" Lin asked, somewhat sceptically.

"I feel greatly honoured to be able to say that I like reading just as much as you do, novels, poetry, even fairy tales. Before Liberation, my favourite was Turgenev and by the fifth grade I had already read *A Nest of Gentlefolk*. The old German Lemm used to make me cry. I also liked Elena but Insalov was not well depicted. However, there is something fresh and pure and full of lyricism in his writing."

He suddenly walked over to where Lin was sitting. Supporting himself on the back of the sofa he went on, "I still enjoy reading. It's like entering a dream world, but when you've finished it just fades away." He moved around and sat next to Lin, his eyes half-shut again. "When I read a good novel I dream of seeing a pure, wonderful, lucid world. I want to go and be a sailor or put on a white lab coat and do research on red blood cells, or become a gardener and grow rare flowers." He laughed as Lin had never heard him laugh before. It seemed to come straight from the heart. "Instead I have to continue being head of the organization department." He shrugged.

"Why do you feel that your work now is so different from the world you find in novels? Isn't working for the Party pure, wonderful and lucid?" Lin asked.

Liu Shiwu shook his head, coughed and stood up again. He moved a little distance away and said sarcastically: "It's not appropriate for Party workers to read novels. For instance," he waved his hand in the air, "take the recruitment of Party members. Just think what a novel would say: 'Long live the many new fighters who have joined lines of the proletarian vanguard in our glorious cause!' And then look at the organization department's real concerns: an organization member of some Party branch is sloppy and unable to give us a clear summary of a new Party member's records. Or we're sitting on more than a hundred applications to join the Party with no time to go through them all. Or maybe new Party members are needing the approval of the standing committee but the moment the committee members hear there is going to be a meeting to do this they all ask for leave. Or people nod off to sleep during the meeting. . . ."

"You're wrong!" Lin contested angrily, as indignant as if he himself had been insulted. "You don't see the real glorious cause. You only see people dozing off. Maybe you even drop off to sleep yourself!"

Liu Shiwu laughed and called out to Han Changxin: "Come and take a look at the last moves of this game in the paper. What do you think? Should the rook or the knight move first?"

9

Wei Heming told Lin Zhen that he wanted to go back to being a worker again. "I can't handle being a branch committee member and a production section chief." Lin disagreed violently, urging him instead to send the opinions collected at the meeting to the Party newspaper. "You're giving up, aren't you? You don't have any faith left in the Party and the country any more, do you?"

Eventually Wei and a few of the more outspoken workers wrote a long letter, which they then sent secretly to the *Beijing Daily*. Wei Heming was uncertain whether or not they had taken the right course of action. "Perhaps this counts as 'cliquism' too. Well, if it does, then let them punish me for it!" Despite this, he felt rather guilty as he posted the letter.

In mid-May the *Beijing Daily* gave a prominent place to this letter from the rank-and-file attacking the bureaucratism of Wang Qingquan. The "Letter from a Group of Workers at the Tonghua Gunny Sack Factory" angrily demanded that action should be taken. An editorial said: "The relevant authorities should make a thorough investigation immediately. . . ."

Zhao Huiwen was the first to discover the letter and she instantly called Lin over to read it. Lin, hands trembling in excitement, looked at it for a long time without quite taking it in. "Good!" he thought, "something's happening at last!"

He gave the paper to Liu Shiwu who read it carefully several times. Waving the paper in the air he said unemotionally: "Well, the gloves are off now!"

Zhou Runxiang, the district Party committee secretary came in. "Do you know anything about this Wang Qingquan business?"

Liu replied calmly: "Well, its's true that the sack factory Party branch does have its problems. We've looked into this before and not so long ago I went to have a talk with Wang Qingquan myself, and young Comrade Lin here went to have a look at the situation too." He turned to Lin, "What do you think about Wang?"

There was a knock on the door and Wei rushed in, his normally ruddy complexion drained of colour. He said that Manager Wang had become extremely angry after seeing the newspaper and was trying to find out who'd written the letter.

Much to Lin's surprise, Liu Shiwu set about dealing with the factory's problems with unexpected speed and efficiency. Once he had made up his mind about something, he was extremely competent in whatever he did. Delegating all of his other duties, he and Lin went to the factory several days in succession. Familiarising himself with the situation on the shop floor first, he then made a detailed investigation of Wang Qingquan's work style and listened carefully to the factory workers' opinions. He consulted all of the relevant departments and settled the case within a week. The Party and administrative bodies all recommended Wang's dismissal.

The meeting held concerning Wang Qingquan continued deep into the night. It was raining intermittently when it finally broke up, and a chilly wind was blowing. Liu Shiwu and Lin went off together to a snack bar to have some dumpling soup.

The café was a recently opened joint state-private venture. Inside, it was neat and pleasant. Customers were few because of the rain. They skirted round the stove and sat down at a table in the corner.

Having placed their order, Liu decided to have a drink as well. He took a sip and then, calculating on his fingers, said with emotion, "This is the sixth time I've been involved in disciplining cadres who've stepped out of line. The first few times I was very depressed about it." His voice was hoarse from having spoken so animatedly at the meeting, "Party workers are like doctors. Their job is to cure people, but they never get any relaxation themselves." He drummed his fingers lightly on the table.

Lin nodded in agreement.

"What's the date today?" asked Liu suddenly.

"The twentieth of May."

"The twentieth of May. . . . Nine years ago today I was wounded in the leg fighting the Kuomintang 208th Youth Division."

"You were wounded?" Lin realized how little he knew about Liu's past.

Liu did not reply. Outside, the rain became heavier. He listened to its rhythmic pattering and could smell the damp earth. A small child suddenly came racing in, his hair dripping.

Liu Shiwu called over to the waiter. "Bring us some lean pork, will you!"

He turned back to Lin. "In 1947 I was chairman of the Students Self-government Committee at Beijing University. I took part in the May 20th demonstration and some thugs from the 208th Division wounded me in the leg. He rolled up his trouser leg to reveal a crescent-shaped scar and then stood up. "See, my left leg's a little shorter than my right."

Lin looked at him with respect and affection for the first time.

Liu's face became flushed as he drank. He sat down and gave Lin some pork. Cocking his head to one side, he said, "How dedicated I used to be in those days. I was so young. How I wish I could. . . ."

"Aren't you any more?"

"Of course not," he replied, toying with his empty cup. "I'm just so busy that work now seems routine and tiring. I haven't slept longer than eight hours a night since Liberation. I've dealt with all sorts of people, but I've never had any time to deal with myself." He rested his chin in his hand and looked Lin straight in the eye. "To be a Bolshevik you must have broad experience and also remain uncorrupted in your thinking. Another please. . . ." he said, holding his cup out to the waiter.

Lin had found himself moved by this profound sincerity. Liu continued sombrely, "They say one of the occupational diseases of being a cook is that you lose your appetite from being around food all day long. We Party workers have created a new way of life but in the end we ourselves don't seem to be able to appreciate it."

Lin was about to say something when Liu Shiwu stopped him with a wave of his hand, indicating that he wasn't in the mood for a discussion. Silent, he stared blankly, his chin cupped in his hands.

"It's not raining so hard now. This rain will be good for the crops." After another long silence he sighed and suddenly said, "You're a good cadre — better than Han Changxin."

Lin, confused, gulped his soup down.

Liu looked at him and said with a warm smile, "How is Zhao Huiwen these days?"

"She's fine," came the casual reply. Lin reached out to pick up some meat with his chopsticks and caught Liu Shiwu's eyes firmly fixed on him.

Liu Shiwu brought his chair closer to Lin's and said

slowly, "Forgive my frankness, but I feel I ought to tell you. . . ."

"Tell me what?" Lin stopped eating.

"It seems to me that there's something about Zhao's feelings for you that. . . ."

His hand trembling, Lin lay down his chopsticks.

By the time they left the café, the rain had already stopped. Stars were beginning to appear from behind the dark clouds and the wind was colder. Rainwater gurgled along the roadside gutters. Lin rushed back to his dormitory in a state of confusion, as if he rather than Liu Shiwu had been drinking. All his roommates were sound asleep and all he could hear was the sound of rhythmic snoring. Lin sat on his bed and felt his wet trouser cuffs. Zhao's beautiful pale face floated before his eyes. He felt young and inexperienced. Walking over to the window, he pressed his face against the cold, rain-spattered glass.

10

The District Party Committee convened a meeting of the members of its standing committee on the issue of the gunny sack factory.

Lin Zhen was specially invited to attend the meeting. He sat in a corner nervously, his heart pounding, his palms sweating. In his pocket were the notes for a long speech in which he was going to use the sack factory incident as a starting point for talking about problems in the organization department itself. He felt that the case of the sack factory provided the right sort of impetus for getting the leadership to take a good hard look at the organization department's work. And now the time had come.

Liu Shiwu was giving a methodical report on the situation. Secretary Zhou rested his broad, strong face on his left hand. His right hand lay on a piece of paper, and he occasionally made notes. Li Zongqin was writing in the air with his index finger. Han Changxin was preoccupied in tying and untying his shoelaces.

Lin wanted to speak on several occasions but his heart was pounding so much that he could hardly breathe. This was the first time he had attended a standing committee meeting. Perhaps it was presumptuous of him to plan to make such a bold speech. He told himself not to be afraid. He remembered when he was eight years old learning how to dive in Qingdao. At that time too he had heard his heart pounding and had angrily told himself not to be frightened.

The standing committee passed Liu Shiwu's proposals on the sack factory problem and wanted to move straight on to the next item on the agenda, but Lin raised his hand.

"It's not necessary to raise your hand when you want to say something," said Secretary Zhou with a smile.

Lin's chair scraped noisily as he stood up. Afraid to look at the people around him, he stared fixedly down at his notes.

"Wang Qingquan has been dealt with, but how can we guarantee that this won't happen again. We must examine the shortcomings of the District Party Committee's organizational work. Firstly, we're only concerned with the work of Party building but we don't pay proper attention to the consolidation of the Party. Instead we allow internal struggles at the grass roots level to go undirected. Secondly, we are all aware that there are problems, but we have put off dealing with them. Take Wang Qingquan for example. He had been at the gunny sack factory for five years and the problem just got more and more serious all the time. Frankly, I feel that Comrade Han Changxin and Comrade Liu Shiwu bear the responsibility for this. . . ."

There was a general rustling throughout the hall. Some people coughed, some put down their cigarettes, others opened their notebooks and a few shifted their chairs.

Han shrugged his shoulders and ran his tongue over his teeth. He said sarcastically, "It's always easy to be wise after the event and of course the earlier something is dealt with the better. What's more, there's no way that the organization department can guarantee that this sort of thing won't happen again. Not even Comrade Lin can guarantee that. . . ."

Lin raised his head and glared at Han Changxin who smiled coldly in response. Lin collected himself: "Comrade Han knows that it's axiomatic that shortcomings exist but he seems to be unaware that it is even more axiomatic to overcome them. Both Comrade Han and Director Liu embrace the former and consequently condone extremely serious shortcomings." He wiped his brow. He hadn't anticipated being so outspoken, but now he felt relieved.

Li Zongqin's finger stopped in mid-air. Zhou Runxiang looked at Lin, and then at the audience. His heavy frame made the chair creak. He asked Liu Shiwu, "What's your opinion?"

Liu nodded, "What Comrade Lin Zhen says is correct and his enthusiastic attitude is inspiring. . . ." He ambled over to the table to get some tea before continuing pensively, "But it's difficult to arrive at a precise understanding of the sack factory affair. He's right. The organization department does not do enough to consolidate the Party — we don't have enough cadres to recruit new members. However it must be said that the case of Wang Qingquan was dealt with speedily and effectively. When the announcement was made at the meeting, workers' feelings reached an unprecedented level. Even some of the more backward workers became more fully aware of the Party's impartiality. One of the old workers got up on the platform in tears, and reiterated their gratitude to the Party and the District Party Committee. . . ."

Lin Zhen said in a low voice, "Exactly. And it's precisely because of this that I feel that our apathy, procrastination and irresponsibility is a crime against the masses." He raised his voice, "The Party belongs to the people, and is the heart of the people. In the same way that we cannot allow dust on the heart, we cannot tolerate shortcomings within Party organizations."

Folding his hands on his knees, Li Zongqin spoke slowly, choosing his words with care, "I think that there are two major points at issue in this debate between Lin and Han and Liu. The first is the clash between regulation and initiative. The second is. . . ."

Lin, surprised at his own audacity, interrupted, "I hope this won't be just a 'rational and comprehensive analysis'. . . ." Afraid that he might burst into tears he stopped short.

Zhou looked at Lin Zhen, then at Li Zongqin and frowned. He remained silent for a while and jotted down a few notes, then said, "Let's go on to the next item."

After the meeting finished, Lin Zhen was so angry that he couldn't eat. He'd never thought it possible that the secretary might have such an attitude. He felt resentful and even rather disappointed. Han and Liu sought him out to take a walk as if nothing had happened between them, reinforcing Lin's realization of their difference in status. He smiled bitterly at himself: "You're naive enough to think that all it takes is to give a speech at the standing committee meeting and everything will be sorted out!" He opened his drawer and took out the Soviet novel which Han had jeered at and turned to the title page on which was written. "Live your life as Nastya does!" "But that's really difficult," he said to himself.

What was it that he lacked?

II

The following day after work, Zhao Huiwen came up to him. "I've made some dumplings. Why don't you come to my place for supper?" He wanted to decline, but she had already left.

Lin hesitated a long time before deciding to eat in the canteen and visit Zhao Huiwen afterwards. Just as he arrived the dumplings were ready. Zhao was wearing a dark red cheongsam with an apron and her hands were covered with flour. She said graciously: "I got fresh kidney beans for the stuffing. . . ."

Lin said haltingly, "I've already had my supper."

Refusing to accept this, she went to get some chopsticks. Lin reiterated that he had eaten and Zhao had no choice but to start eating by herself. Lin sat uncomfortably to one side, looking restlessly round the room, rubbing his hands and shifting about nervously.

"Lin, is there something wrong?" Zhao stopped eating.

"No. . . ."

"Come on, tell me." Zhao's eyes didn't leave his face.

"Yesterday at the standing committee meeting I told them what I thought, but Secretary Zhou didn't pay any attention. . . ."

Zhao nibbled thoughtfully on the end of her chopsticks. Then she said firmly: "No, it wouldn't be that. It's just that Comrade Zhou Runxiang doesn't give his opinions lightly. . . ."

"Maybe," he said somewhat doubtfully, his head lowered, not daring to meet Zhao's warm gaze.

Zhao ate a few more dumplings. "Is there anything else?"

Lin's heart was pounding. He raised his head and saw Zhao's friendly expression. He said quietly, "Comrade Zhao. . . ."

She put down her chopsticks and leaned against the chair, looking slightly surprised.

"I would very much like to know whether you are happy or not." Lin's voice took on a grave, adult tone. "When I first arrived I saw you crying in Liu Shiwu's office. I didn't think any more about it after that. I just went along in my own way not really thinking about others. Tell me, are you happy?"

Zhao looked at him rather uncertainly and shook her head. "Sometimes I forget too. . . ." Then she nodded, "Yes, it's possible to be happy. Why are you asking me?" She smiled calmly.

"Forgive me, I'd like to tell you about something that Liu Shiwu brought up. It's all nonsense really. . . . I like spending time with you talking and listening to music. You're a very nice person. . . . It's natural, not at all surprising. But perhaps there is something wrong or improper about this or maybe I'm placing too much emphasis on it. I'm always afraid of upsetting other people," he concluded apologetically.

Zhao continued smiling calmly, her eyebrows slightly raised. She lifted her slender arm, rubbed her forehead and then shook her head and turned away as if trying to get rid of some unwelcome thought. She walked slowly over to the newly-hung oil painting and stood looking at it silently. The picture was entitled *Spring*. It was Moscow, with spring sunlight just appearing and a mother and child walking along a street. . . .

She turned back and went to sit on the bed. Her hand resting on the bedrail she said quietly, "Just what do you think you are saying? I certainly wouldn't do anything rash. I have a husband and a child to think about. I still haven't told you about my husband." The word "husband" sounded almost formal. "I got married in 1952 when I was only nineteen. I should never have got married so young. He was transferred from the army to become a section chief in one of the big ministries. Bit by bit he changed and became a real climber. He started pushing for improved status and better treatment and wouldn't co-operate with others. All that's left between us now is that he comes home on Saturday nights and leaves again Monday mornings. For me, it's either got to be true love or nothing at all. We've had our arguments but I still wait for him. He's in Shanghai at the moment and when he gets back I intend to have a proper talk with him." Then she asked again, "What were you trying to say, Lin? You're a very good friend and I respect you very much, but you are still just a child. I'm sorry if calling you that upsets you. We all want to lead the right kind of life and we all hope that the department will be the right kind of Party work organization. You're just like a brother to me, and I know you want me to be more assertive. People should be friendly and support one another. I always hate unfriendliness. But it's not more than that. What else could there be?"

"I shouldn't have been so influenced by Liu Shiwu. . . ." said Lin regretfully.

Zhao shook her head. "Liu Shiwu is an intelligent man. Who can say that his warning was not entirely out of place?" She sighed deeply. "So that's that."

She picked up the bowl and chopsticks and left the room. Lin jumped up and began pacing up and down thoughtfully. At first it seemed that there was still much to be said but gradually he could find nothing at all. After all, nothing had happened. Life sometimes brought a current of feeling which moved or troubled you and then flowed out again leaving no trace . . . but was there really no trace? It left a pure and beautiful memory, indistinct but indelible.

Zhao Huiwen returned leading her two-year-old son and carrying a bag. The child had seen Lin many times before and greeted him with affection.

Lin lifted him up in his strong arms. Suddenly the room echoed with the sound of the child's laughter.

Zhao took a file out of the bag. "This evening I want you to take a look at something. I've made some notes on my observations of problems in the organization department over the last three years."

She picked up a piece of graph paper. "This might seem a bit laughable to you. I've set a sort of contest for myself, comparing my work yesterday with my work today. I've drawn up a chart and if I've made a mistake, for instance copied out an applicant's name wrongly or miscalculated the number of new Party members, I put a big black cross on it. If I haven't made any mistakes all day I put in a little red flag. If I manage to have only red flags for a whole month then I go out and buy a pretty scarf or something else as a reward. Perhaps this seems a bit childish to you."

Lin, engrossed, replied, "Not in the least. I respect the way you. . . ."

It was dark when Lin left. They stood in the doorway. Her eyes glinting in the darkness, Zhao said, "Isn't it a beautiful night tonight? Can you smell the scholartree. Just ordinary little white flowers, yet they are more elegant than the peony and more fragrant than peaches or plums. You can't smell them? Really? Well, I must say good night. I'll see you tomorrow morning when we can throw ourselves once again into our vital if at times tedious work. After work, you can come over and we can listen to that wonderful *Capriccio Italien.* Then I'll cook some water chestnuts and we can throw the skins onto the floor. . . ."

Lin Zhen leaned against the pillar in front of the organization department gate for a long time, looking up at the night sky. An early summer breeze was blowing gently — it had been winter when he arrived and now it was already the beginning of summer. He had passed his first spring at the District Party Committee.

He had achieved very little, almost nothing, but he had learned a lot. He had come to understand much more, to realize the real beauty of life and its real significance. He had come to understand the hardship and value of struggle. He had gradually learned that in this ordinary, yet still praiseworthy, overworked and all-embracing District Party Committee, it was impossible to rely on the courage of one person alone to achieve anything. . . . From tomorrow onwards. . . .

One of his colleagues called out as he went past, "Where are you off to, Lin? Go and see Comrade Zhou Runxiang. He's asked for you three times already."

The District Party Committee secretary was looking for him? So it wouldn't be tomorrow but tonight that he would try his best to obtain guidance from the leadership. This was of vital importance at present. . . .

Through the office window, he could see the green lamp and the large shadow of the District Party secretary. With determination, he knocked impatiently on the door of the leading comrade's office.

Translated by Alison Bailey and Carole Murray

王 蒙 小 说 选

熊 猫 丛 书

*

《中国文学》雜誌社出版

（中国北京百万庄路24号）

外文印刷厂印刷

中国国际书店发行

1983年（36开）第1版

编号：（英）2—916—20

00160

10—E—1636P